THE TAKE OVER

JT LEATH

ACKNOWLEDGEMENTS

First off, I want to thank God for all my many blessings because through all my trials and tribulations life has taught me a lesson. God blessed me with the unique gift to be a writer, so I'll give it my all. Next, I want to thank my future wife Sheryl for sticking by my side and not giving up on me when time got hard. For that very reason I just want to say thank you and I love you. To my son Aiden, just know that daddy loves you with all his heart. No matter what you may hear about me, please know that yo daddy was a gangsta and he still always thought of you. I'll never stop loving you. To my unborn seeds, until life brings you forth, I'll keep pushing this pen and writing this Real 2 Life shit. To all my readers, I want to thank ya'll for supporting me in my line of work. Thank you because if it wasn't for me you guys there would be no me, so I'm going to give ya'll everything I got through my writings and story telling's. To my real niggas locked away, especially the ones who believed in me when I first started writing Sleep, Freddie, and Zoe J-P. Ya'll keep ya'll eyes open and ya'll heads up. Also, anybody else I did time with... ya'll back that up because ya'll was the ones who pushed me every day. I am grateful.

Sheryl, the struggle is finally over baby. Now it's time to collect and get this real money!

DEDICATION

This book is dedicated to my grandma, Willie Mae Roberts and my mother, Danica Ann Thomas. I love and miss ya'll so much. Words can't begin to express how badly I feel from losing ya'll. But I want to let ya'll know that I did something productive with myself for once other than catching cases out here on these streets. Also, to my grandad Herbert Roberts, I love you always and I know you are smiling down on me from up above. Grandad please keep me covered and continue to watch over me. You guys will always be in my heart. My only mission is to make ya'll proud and hopefully with this, I accomplished it.

The Beginning
CHAPTER 1

It was summertime in the state of Florida, known as "The sunshine state." I was in Broward County in the city of Fort Lauderdale.

School was out for the ones that attended which was a very low percentage. They came from an environment known as the ghetto. Everywhere you turned and looked you had black kids standing on the street corners from all ages. It didn't matter what time of the day, even throughout the wee hours of the morning in every neighborhood, you'll find them posted up.

As far as the parks, well that's where everything went down. Drugs were being sold to the crackheads on the block. You even had prostitutes of all ages, starting from as young as twelve and thirteen years old. They sold pussy for a cheap ass twenty dollars round the clock.

This was Fort Lauderdale at its best. This is what goes on in black communities on a regular basis. So, seeing this was a regular thing around here. Especially for young black kids hanging out at the parks.

There was a five-on-five whole court game going on at the park in the hood called Washington Park, and everybody was watching. Even the up and comings who were on the sideline shooting dices.

K-Dog and Killa were best friends who were clicked tight, both were fearless men. They were also hustlers, but most of all, they were some ruthless muthafuckas.

K-Dog was a pro when it came down to shooting dice. He knew how to manipulate the dice and make them do what he wanted them to do. That was his gift and it worked like magic.

One of the youngsters who were amongst the crowd decided he wanted to join the dice game. Now shooting against K-Dog, jit became 38 hot at the fact that he was losing all his money. That's when he made an outburst that made K-Dog feel some type of way.

"Nigga who you think you talking to like that?" K-Dog said, getting back in the youngster's face.

"I'm talking to you, with your cheating ass," the jit responded back to K-Dog, showing no weakness. That was the worst mistake he made. Rule #1: never go in somebody else's hood and talk shit, especially K-Dog; he was the wrong nigga to fuck with.

Before K-Dog could say or do anything, Killa came out of nowhere and delivered a punch that was so powerful when it connected. He hit the youngster dead in the nose. It looked like his head exploded, sending blood everywhere. The youngster was already sleep before he hit the pavement, and when he did, Killa started stomping on the kid's face like he was tap dancing. All you can hear was the "ohhs and ahh" from the rest of the kids at the park as they witnessed the beat down.

Before Killa could do any serious damage than he already done, K-Dog jumped in, pulling Killa off the youngster. "That's enough, bruh, the nigga is unconscious. What you tryna do nigga, catch a body?" K-Dog said.

"Nigga, if you didn't stop me, I would've!" Killa replied while looking K-Dog dead in the eyes. All K-Dog could do was shake his head at Killa because he knew he meant every word.

"Come on, nigga; let's go before someone calls the police," K-Dog said while turning around and pulling Killa by the arm.

"Hold up, bruh. Hold up!" Killa said while pulling away.

"What bruh?"

"Hold on, nigga, damn." Killa walked back to where the youngster was laying down, still unconscious on the pavement and kicked him one last time before turning around and walking toward K-Dog. "Nigga now we can go," Killa said.

Kenny "K-Dog" Williams was only eighteen years old at that time. This young nigga was swift and a smooth talker also. Especially when it came to older women, he had a thing for cougars. He was laid back and smarter than the average 18-year-old. Even in school, he passed every subject with flying colors. K-Dog was not only book smart, but street smart as well. People called him a young master mind because he was one of a kind.

As for Killa, he was labeled a problem child and very rough around the edges. Since he was fourteen years old, growing up, Killa was in and out of the juvenile detention center. He also had a bad anger problem. His temper would shoot from 0 to 100 really quick. Killa was only a year younger than K-Dog. His mother was on crack bad and his father was serving a life sentence in prison, on three counts of attempted murder. Growing up was hard without a father figure around. He was no different from the other children that were raised by a single parent. This was a common thing in the black communities.

After leaving the park, both K-Dog and Killa decided to hit the block, leaving the crowd to attend to the injured boy that would soon become their enemy. They were headed towards 7th CT. It wasn't too far away from the park, just a couple blocks away.

Killa then reached into his pockets and pulled out a brand-new pack of Backwoods and passed it to K-Dog. "Here, bruh."

Grind Mode
Killa
CHAPTER 2

Killa was inside his room, bagging up dope, when his room door flew open. "Keith, baby could you…" his mother stop dead in her tracks while looking at the cut rocks Killa had scattered all over his bed.

"Ma, I told you about walking in my room when my room door is closed!"

"I'm sorry, baby. Mama just wanted to know if you got some money, so I can put some food in the house… that's all, baby."

Even though Killa's mother was strung out on drugs, Killa still treated her with the utmost respect. Even when she got on his last nerve, Killa made sure he looked out for her; she was all that he had left.

Killa got up and grabbed a shoe box from out of his closet and took out $400. He gave it to her.

"Here, Ma."

"Thank you, mamas' baby," she said, taking the money.

"Thank you, my behind. Don't let me find out you out here spending my money on that shit," Killa said, looking her dead in her eyes.

"Boy, hush! I got dis," his mother said before walking out of Killa's room, closing the door behind her.

Thirty minutes later, Killa was walking out the front door with a pocket full of rocks and his Glock 40 that was tucked on his waistline. Killa was 6'1" and weighed 195 pounds. He was pure muscle. His complexion was a dark brown color. He was only seventeen years old with a mouth full of golds and a head full of dreads.

The only thing that was on Killa's mind as he was walking towards his girl's car, was how he was gonna get this money. The apartment complex building they were at only had six doors. Three on the bottom floor and three on the top floor. It was old and run down. It didn't matter what time of the day it was, crack smokers were standing out front.

Just as Killa was opening the driver side door to get in, a crackhead named Pam approached him.

"Hey, auntie baby," Pam said, standing in her used to be sexy stance.

"Oh, waz good, Pam?"

"You good, right?" Pam said, referring to her medication… crack.

"Yeah, I'm good. Waz up?" Killa said, getting into the vehicle.

"Boy, I wanna fat ass twenty," Pam said, looking around, tryna be slick. She didn't want the other smokers that were standing there being nosy to see her buying dope.

Pam reached into her dirty bra, pulling out a balled up twenty-dollar bill and gave it to Killa, in exchange for a twenty piece.

"Here you go, Pam," Killa said, passing her a nice sized rock for the dub.

"Thank you, nephew," Pam said as she got excited.

"When I get sum moe money, I'ma holla at cha... okay?" Pam walked off, not giving Killa time to respond.

"Ay, Pam, I saw that," another smoker said while walking behind her.

"This is my first piece of the day, and I ain't got shit fa nobody," Pam said, walking towards her apartment while digging in her ass. It looked dirty too.

Killa shook his head and started heading back towards the block... 7th CT. When Killa pulled up on the block, he parked next to an old lady house. Her name was Ms. B. Killa got out the car and walked up to where K-Dog was posted up with a group of niggas, shooting dice. He gave his right-hand man dap.

"Wat they do, bruh-bruh?" Killa said.

"Shiiddd... you already know, bruh. I'm tryna break these niggas," K-Dog responded, holding a whole bunch of money in his hand.

K-Dog was talking to Killa and shooting dice at the same time, talking cash shit. A car pulled up with four girls that had the music blasting.

"Cheeze in da trap!" one of the youngsters yelled. That's all it took for somebody to yell, before the whole car was surrounded.

K-Dog and Killa was on beat, when the chicks pulled up. One rushed the driver side while the other one went to the passenger. They had to stick and move, get in and get out. They got their numbers and fell back.

Killa and K-Dog took turns serving, one would watch for 5-o while the other one served. They had everything down pack all the way down to the T. And when they moved, they moved in a unit... as one! These two youngsters had formed a bond that was based on loyalty. And loyalty was a solid foundation to have in this environment. They both had a role to play. K-Dog was the master mind and Killa was the muscle.

***

11:38pm...

For eight hours straight, the youngsters did their thing. 7th CT was a gold mind when it came to making money. But at the same time if you didn't know the game and you came around there thinking shit was peaches and cream, then you were sadly mistaken.

Ms. B had been around for a while since the early 80's. She'd been living on 7th CT in the same house for as long as they could remember. Ms. B was as cool as a fan on a summer day and she was down for her peoples. She was one of those types who loved to smoke weed, talk cash shit, and most important she loved to get money.

Everybody gave Ms. B respect. She was like everybody's grandma. Ms. B cooked food for them and all; that real soul food. She sold five-dollar plates, shots of liquor, and she had a store house too. Ms. B was a one stop shop. Get it and go.

Killa and K-Dog was sitting on Ms. B's porch, listening to her kick that fly shit about how it was back in the days, when Killa's' girlfriend, Precious. walked out of her grandma's door.

"Bae, I'm ready to go," she said, interrupting her grandma as she was on the verge of getting to the good part of her story.

"Chile! You don't see me tellin em' my story, on how shit was back in the days," Ms. B said, passing K-Dog the blunt.

"Grandma, don't nobody care about how it was way way way back in the days," Precious said with her hands on her hips while giving Killa that 'nigga, let's go look.'

"Damn," Killa said before getting up.

"Wat you fena do, bruh?" Killa said to K-Dog.

"Go head, bruh. I'ma chill for a minute or two."

"You sho, fam?" Killa responded.

"Yeah, man." K-Dog stood up, giving his right-hand man dap.

"Be safe, bruh." Killa turned around and walked off.

"That chile think she run sum'thin. She lucky that ain't me, I'd tell her 'bout herself," Ms. B said as Killa and Precious walked towards Precious' car.

***

Killa decided to go to Precious' place since she was complaining about him not spending enough time with her. Besides, he knew Precious wanted some of him and he was in the mood too. Precious was twenty-one years old and she had her shit together. She worked at Bell South which was a major well-known phone company. Precious had her own vehicle and she had a nice 2-bedroom condo out in Coral Springs.

Anybody that knew about Coral Springs, they knew the cost of living in that area wasn't cheap at all. Everything about Precious was high maintenance. From her bra to her underwear, even the clothes she put on her back had to be name brand. Truth be told ever since Precious was born into this world, her father, who was a dope boy, spoiled her. Precious never dealt with somebody younger than her, let alone been into a relationship with them. Precious always preferred older guys because they weren't about too many games, but she couldn't help herself after laying eyes on Killa. It was something different about him. He reminded her of her father before he was murdered.

Precious had just exited the bathroom while walking into her bedroom still damp, wrapped in her favorite towel Killa had bought her a year ago. She didn't waste no time letting the towel unravel and fall to the carpet.

"Damn," Killa said to himself, looking Precious up and down, she had a body of a stripper... straight flawless.

Precious was super horny as she climbed into the king-sized bed while reaching for Killa's pants, unbuttoning them in one motion. She was glad to see that Killa's dick was already on hard when she pulled it out of his pants.

"Umm... I see somebody missed me," Precious said, putting the tip of his dick into the warmth of her mouth, while holding eye contact with him, slowly blowing Killa's mind away.

For ten minutes straight, Precious performed the best oral sex he'd ever gotten. Her head game was wicked. It was like she was sucking his soul right out of his body.

"Fuck me, baby," Precious stated as she got on all fours.

This was Killa's favorite position, he wasted no time getting behind Precious' rear end, slowly inserting his stiff dick into her wet garden.

She arched her back a little, preparing herself for what this young stud was about to put on her... The Pound Game.

Killa grabbed both of Precious's ass cheeks, spreading them wide as they could go, while fucking her with deep long strokes. Killa was hitting the bottom of Precious's ocean, applying straight pressure. It was like Killa tried to dig a grave up by how much pressure he was applying.

"Oooh, shit, bae... that's right... beat dis pussy... beat dis pussy!" Precious yelled out while throwing it back, meeting Killa thrust for thrust.

"Grab me by da throat and pull my hair really hard bae." Precious was a lady in the streets, but in the sheets, she was a straight up freak.

Killa did everything Precious asked him to do and every desire her body craved for... and he meant everything! Precious lost count how many times she came. It was crazy how Killa was dicking her down, mixing pleasure with pain.

Killa had Precious legs behind her head, acting a donkey while he stood up in that pussy, Killa was preforming like the champ he was. At 6'1" and blessed with a dick of a grown man that was big enough to drive the average woman insane. Could you imagine?

"Ooh, shit, bae… I'm fena nutt," Killa said, speeding up while holding Precious legs up in the air by her ankles. Those words were like magic to her ears as she took in every inch, he was able to produce.

"Ooh, shit! Ooh, shit!" Killa snatched his dick out of Precious's wet juices and busted all over her flat stomach.

"Yes, yes, yes… ooh, yes" Precious was rubbing Killa's nut, smearing it all over her stomach and private parts, while at the same time, stroking Killa's dick.

"Killa, you know I love you, right?" Precious said while wiping herself off.

This was Precious way of expressing the love she has for him. Killa had totally opened Precious heart, piercing it to the core.

"Why you trippin, girl? You already know I know," Killa said, laying down.

"Come on, get in bed, so we can lay down, because tomorrow I got a long day."

The Plot
Three Months Later
K-Dog
CHAPTER 3

K-Dog was at the park in the hood, talking to a lil' freak named Indian. Nothing was special about her other than what was between her legs, that patch of hair made a lotta niggas go crazy over her. Indian was nineteen and already had two kids from two different baby daddies, which of course were best friends. One of the reasons why K-Dog dealt with her was because she had a vehicle and Indian didn't mind taking him to bust his licks.

While K-Dog was talking to Indian, tryna get some head outta her, his cell phone started going off.

"Hello," he answered it.

"K-Dog this Tom."

"Wuz up, Tom?"

"Are you in the area?" Tom asked.

"Yeah, I'm in da hood at Washington Park."

"Ima need a $60."

"Slide at the park, I gotcha."

"Aiight, bud. I'm on my way."

K-Dog ended the call and continued talking to Indian. "So, what you gonna do, give me sum neck or wat?"

"Boy, you got peoples already," Indian said, tryna play hard to get.

"What that got to do with anything?" K-Dog said, stroking her backside.

"Nothin', I'm just sayin'."

"Aight, then. I'll call you later on," K-Dog said, cutting her off mid-sentence as he walked off. Tom had just pulled up, parking not too far from where K-Dog was standing, Tom blew his horn, getting K-Dog's attention. After going to his bomb, K-Dog walked towards Tom's vehicle and opened the passenger door.

"Hey, buddy!" Tom said excited.

"Wuz good, Tom?"

"You know working and shit." Tom passed the money to K-Dog, hoping he would put it in his pockets and not count it. But to his surprise K-Dog started counting it before turning towards Tom.

"Dis $50, Tom; you ten short."

"I know, bud, I'm sorry. Shit ain't going right with me and Melisa. But look I will make it up, I promise."

K-Dog knew Tom was running game, so he let him slide.

"No problem, Tom, you gud." K-Dog gave him the dope and got out.

"Alright, pal, be safe" Tom said, pulling off.

Right when K-Dog was walking towards the group of thugs shooting CeeLo—three dice—Killa pulled up in Precious' BMW and got out.

"Wuz up, fool?" K-Dog yelled as Killa approached him.

"Wuz poppin', nigga?" Killa said, giving K-Dog dap.

"Money, nigga, you already know. Slide over here and

watch how I break deez niggas," Killa and K-Dog walked over to the dice game.

"What's in the bank?" K-Dog asked.

"$200!" said the bank man.

"It stopped… nigga, shoot." K-Dog pulled out a bank-roll and threw down ten twenties.

The bank man picked up all three dices and shook 'em up.

"Point on dis nigga he said while rolling the dices"

"Dick nigga… 123!" K-Dog said, calling the numbers the dice landed on.

"Dats double!"

"Damn," the bank man said while passing K-Dog $400.

"Thank you." Now K-Dog was the bank man.

"What y'all down?" K-Dog said, getting the bets right while shaking the dices. Once everyone bet was on the line, K-Dog made the dices do magic. When he let them go, he threw big numbers.

"Triple… er'body get naked… y'all get that money right."

An hour later, K-Dog was walking away with $2,400, and the only reason K-Dog was walking away was because he had some information he wanted to tell Killa and if everything went as planned, then the two would become very wealthy young men. Killa and K-Dog were sitting in Precious's vehicle chiefin' on that loud while watching the road, K-Dog thought that this moment was the perfect time to break the news, so he looked over at Killa and said, "Bruh, I got us a lick."

"A lick! Nigga what kind of lick you got?"

"To get rich."

"Rich!" Killa said, looking over at K-Dog with dollar signs in his eyes.

"I'm listenin'," Killa said, giving K-Dog his full undivided attention.

"We gonna rob Pimp for er'thang."

"Pimp! Nigga you tryna get us killed or sumthin', how in the fuck we gonna rob Pimp when he's protected?" Killa couldn't believe what K-Dog just said.

"Bruh, you kiddin', right?"

"Hell, naw I ain't kiddin nigga."

"Bruh, you my nigga until death do us apart, but I ain't tryna end up like buddy who got body bagged." Killa was shaking his head. It was impossible to rob Pimp; he had too many goons, protecting him 24/7.

"Relax, fool; I got this" K-Dog pulled out his cell phone and dialed a number while putting it on speaker phone.

"Hello."

"Wuz up with you, ma? How was yo' day?"

"Aww, my day was nice how about yours?"

"It's always a beautiful day in my neighborhood," K-Dog responded while looking over at Killa who was totally lost by the voice of the other person who was on speaker. Killa knew this was a grown ass woman, and all he had to do was listen.

"So, wuz up?" the woman said.

"I'm callin' 'bout what we talked about a couple of weeks ago."

"Oh, yeah, that's still good on my end. As a matter of fact, Pimp is going to a Young Jeezy concert tomorrow, so be ready."

"And what time?" K-Dog asked.

"1:00 a.m."

"I gotcha, say nomo." K-Dog and the chick made small talk about how they were going to set the lick up. Killa listened very closely to every detail without saying too much. Moments after K-Dog ended the phone call, he looked over at Killa.

"That was Pimp's wife who I just got off the phone with."

"His wife!" Killa said surprised.

"How you manage to get her to set up Pimp, and how you know she ain't tryna set a nigga up to get murked?" Killa was looking puzzled, and a lotta of shit was going through Killa's head; they was planning on hitting the King of the city... Pimp! This was not a small fish, and they were playing with this was a great white shark.

"Easy. I simply followed Pimp and took pictures with his side chicks, and I presented them to her after that, she made me an offer I couldn't refuse. So, I did what I had to do."

"So, when dis shit supposed to go down?"

"Tomorrow at 1:00 a.m. You in or what?"

"Shid, nigga, you know I'm in." Killa reached over and gave K-Dog dap.

***

The Next Day

Everything was in motion. Tonight, was the night for Killa and K-Dog to make their move on Pimp. Killa was inside his room, at his mother's apartment, preparing to get dressed for the night. The time was 9:30 p.m., so Killa had approximately three and a half hours before the show started. Once Killa was dressed in all-black, he set his alarm for 12:30 a.m. In the meantime, Killa decided to rest a little until it was time for him to put in work. It was like as soon as Killa's eyes closed his alarm started going off, waking him right outta his sleep. Killa got up and walked to his closet and retrieved his Glock 40. He cocked it, putting one in the head before walking out of his room door.

K-Dog was at the spot, waiting, when Killa walked up, but Killa didn't know where K-Dog was, so he paced back and forth while looking at his G-shock every second. K-Dog waited for a minute or two before he made himself known, K-Dog hit the bright lights of the vehicle, signaling for Killa.

"Wat da fuck," Killa said to himself as he pulled his fire out and walked towards the vehicle.

"Who da fuck is dat?" Killa gripped the gun that was now in his hand.

"Killa, dis me, nigga!" K-Dog yelled out the window. "Hurry up, nigga, let's go."

Seconds later, Killa walked towards the passenger side of the vehicle and opened the door and got in. "Nigga, you mean to tell me you were sittin' right here dis whole fuckin' time, watchin' me, bruh and did not say a word?" Killa said, looking at all the stuff that was in the back of the van.

"And who van dis is?"

"My uncle. Now sit back and stop askin' me twenty-one questions." K-Dog started up the van. "You ready to get rich nigga, right?"

"Hell yeah!" Killa responded.

"Well, then let's do dis." K-Dog reached over and gave Killa dap before putting the van in drive and pulling off.

Thirty minutes later, K-Dog and Killa was parked down the street from Pimp's crib, watching for anything that might be suspicious. From the looks of it, everything looked good as gold, so K-Dog pulled out his phone and dialed a number, seconds later, he hung up.

"Here, bruh, put deez on." K-Dog passed Killa a pair of gloves and a ski mask. After Killa did what he was told, K-Dog did the same. K-Dog started the van up and drove up to a big ass house, which of course, belonged to Pimp. Shortly after, K-Dog quietly pulled up the garage of Pimp's house.

"You ready, nigga?"

"Yeah, bruh, let's do dis," Killa responded, clutching his fire. With that being said, K-Dog pulled into the garage and waited for Pimp's wife to close the garage back, before jumping out.

"Let's go, bruh," K-Dog said to Killa before closing the driver door while walking towards Pimp's wife.

K-Dog kissed her passionately while feeling up her skirt.

"Come on, sweetie. I don't know how much time we got, so let's get to it."

She led them into their master bedroom, revealing a large safe. K-Dog walked up and tried to open it, but it was lock.

"Wuz da code?"

"I don't know, Pimp never told me the code." Killa looked at K-Dog while shaking his head.

"I got a plan, nobody panic," K-Dog said, getting up, leaving them both.

Moments later, K-Dog returned with a whole bunch of tools, passing a slug hammer to Killa.

"Wat da fuck you want me to do with dis?"

"You da muscle, nigga, you forgot? Now get da beating, my boy," Killa smiled to himself.

Piece of cake, Killa thought to himself.

"Ya'll stand back and watch," Killa said before knocking chunks out the wall.

Killa and K-Dog took turns tryna beat the safe free from outta the wall, which took them forty minutes.

They both grabbed one end and totted it inside the garage where the van was and loaded it in the back. Once everything was squared away, K-Dog pulled out his gun from his waistline and walked over to Pimp's wife and pointed it at her head.

"Baby, what are you doing?" the woman asked, looking confused

"Wat you thought, I was gonna let you come along knowin' you a snake?" K-Dog said, cocking his .45.

"I thought we had a plan."

"We did." K-Dog looked her dead in her eyes. "If you'll cross your husband, what will you do to me?"

"But this is different, baby, I swear. Please, put the gun down and take me with you," the woman said, pleading for her life.

"Da only thing that beats da cross is da double cross," K-Dog said, pulling the trigger, blowing her brains out everywhere. Killa was amazed at how K-Dog just took a life right before his very eyes. Killa never really seen a life being taken in his presence, let alone by his right-hand man.

"Nigga, get in da van and stop looking lost and shit," K-Dog said while hitting the button on the wall, letting the garage up. The only thing going through Killa's mind was the safe and the body that was on the ground.

"Killa... Killa!" K-Dog yelled until Killa turned around.

"Get yo' ass in nigga and let's go." Killa ran around the van like he was flash and got in?

Lil Boosie was playing in the background while K-Dog and Killa were in route, heading towards K-Dog's uncle warehouse. The whole time while they were riding nobody said a word, they both was in deep thought listening to Lil Boosie "The Take Over."

Twenty minutes later, K-Dog was pulling into his uncle's warehouse off Sunrise Blvd and 4th. K-Dog drove around before parking. He looked over at Killa.

"Bruh, we here," K-Dog said, getting out the van and opened the garage up.

"Aye, bruh, get in da driver seat and pull it in." Killa got into the driver seat and pulled the van in. K-Dog closed the garage back and opened the door to the van.

"Get out and help me, with da safe bruh."

"How we gonna get dis bitch open?" Killa asked, looking confused.

"Don't worry about dis, bruh, I got dis." K-Dog went into the back of the van and returned with a portable welder.

"Stand back and watch me work my magic," K-Dog said firing it up. It took K-Dog a whole hour to open the safe up and when he did, both of their eyes got big like golf balls.

Money was packed neat and tight on top of each other; bands on top of bands. It was so much money K-Dog had to grab two money machines.

"Help me take all dis money out, so we can put it thru da money machine."

They both grabbed the money, placing it on the ground next to the money machine. The youngsters started running the cash through the machine which lasted for hours.

$1.5 million was what the money machine kept displaying on the screen, making them very wealthy young men. Killa and K-Dog sat down exhausted next to the money, wiping the sweat from their brows.

"Dawg, I can't believe we have all dis money," K-Dog said.

"I can't either, bruh, we lucky." K-Dog stood up with his pistol.

"Naw nigga we ain't lucky... we blessed."

Eight Years Later
Bossed Up
K-Dog
CHAPTER 4

Since K-Dog and Killa ran up in Pimp's crib and murdered his wife, Pimp couldn't bounce back and he ended up losing everything; nobody respected Pimp let alone feared him. Pimp was no longer the King of the city and his reigning days had expired years ago, thanks to the one and only... K-Dog and Killa.

They were in power now. Taking over Fort Lauderdale, K-Dog was the H.N.I.C. and Killa was second in charge. The two started a powerful organization.

They both had the streets on click/clack, and the crew they put together was a bunch of stone-cold killers. The two of them were distributing keys of cocaine throughout South Florida.

Every weekend, K-Dog and Killa would throw a block party in the hood for the kids, grown-ups, and the elderly were more welcome to come. Food, candy, and soda pops, were given free. Even when Christmas came around, they bought all the kids in the hood bicycles; this was their way of giving back to the community.

K-Dog invested his money in buying vehicles and flipping them, he had an auction license and a nice car lot where he spent most of his time.

K-Dog was sitting in his office when Killa walked in dressed to impressed.

"Wuz up, boss!" Killa walked up to K-Dog, giving him dap.

"Same ole shit just another day," K-Dog responded.

"Well... I stop by to show you deez papers on the vehicles." Killa passed him the papers, which were titles on all the vehicles that they owned. Mercedes, B.W.M'S, Audis, Lexus', and Jaguars were on the list.

"How much did you pay for the vehicles?"

"100K for thirty luxury vehicles... do da math." K-Dog passed the papers back to Killa.

"When are the shipment scheduled to arrive?" K-Dog asked.

"The vehicles are already here; all I have to do is pick 'em up from da port and bring em here." Killa opened the door and walked out. "I got work to handle boss, I'll catch up with you," Killa said over his shoulders.

K-Dog was now twenty-six years old and he was still young and good looking, and all the kids looked up to him and the elderly respected him for the person he was. This young fellow, along with Killa, gave back to the community by setting up events for the younger peers.

For the money, they hit for and got outta Pimp's safe, they split it down the middle. The youngest at that time had bought his mother a four-bedroom house out in Weston, moving her out the hood.

K-Dog had accomplished a lot over the years. He brought his mother a house and he started businesses for black people that didn't have a job. He was able to do it all, but he lacked one thing and that was finding a good woman that was loyal. It was a lot of chicken heads running at K-Dog, hoping but that wasn't something K-Dog wanted. He didn't care how fine they were, he wanted a real woman, a queen, and not somebody who wanted him for his money.

Around 8:00 p.m., K-Dog always closed down his place of business. There were two cars parked to the side as K-Dog approached his all-white Range Rover, but nobody got out or did anything. K-Dog decided to walk where the two vehicles were parked, but to his surprise as he was approaching the vehicles, they pulled off.

Shortly after, K-Dog got in his S.U.V. and he made sure the coast was clear before pulling off. Minutes later, he jumped on I-95, getting in the fast lane. K-Dog accelerated, pushing the Range Rover over the speed limit; he wanted to make sure nobody wasn't following him.

Twenty minutes later, he was pulling up to the Hard Rock Casino; this was another one of his spots where he spent his time at, other than the 5Wcar lot. K-Dog pulled up and jumped out, leaving the vehicle running for the valet. The only thing that was on his mind when he stepped through the doors, was money.

K-Dog strode right up to the poker table that was unlimited and sat down, and the dealer smiled at him.

"Hello there," the young woman said, holding eye contact with him. She was astonishingly beautiful with a perfect set of nice teeth; her hair was long and wavy.

"How you doing, beautiful?" K-Dog responded while pulling out a bankroll of hundred-dollar bills and passed the big faces to her.

"Here you go, Ms. Dominique." K-Dog read her name tag.

Once K-Dog collected his chips and the dealer dealt everybody's hands out, he looked around, observing every player carefully. There wasn't a threat at the poker table, but this old white man who was wearing a cowboy outfit smiled at K-Dog.

The dealer dealt Texas Holder, dealing K-Dog a pair of aces. Once everybody placed their bets, the dealer flipped over the first three cards, which was an ace, a king, and a ten of heart.

It was a total of five people sitting at the poker table, including K-Dog. The first-person checked, sending it to the next person which was the old man. He threw two fifty/dollar chips, the next person called, sending it around to K-Dog.

"I raised with 500," K-Dog said, throwing five one hundred-dollar chips.

Everybody folded except the old man in the cowboy outfit. The next card was a queen of diamond, K-Dog bet $300 and the old man called.

The next card was an ace, but instead of placing the bet, K-Dog checked, just to see what the old man would do. He bet $700, hoping K-Dog wouldn't call. K-Dog knew he had the best hand, so he played a long; $5,380 was a stake.

"I call, old timer; turn out and win." The old man threw down a queen of spade and a jack of diamond.

"I got a high flush," the old man said, looking over a K-Dog who wasn't showing no emotions.

"I got poker with aces." K-Dog dropped his pair of aces that matched the two on the board. The old man shook his head and got up from the table and shook K-Dog's hand.

"Good game, young blood. I'll see you another time." With that, he walked off. K-Dog won a total of $12,860 just off the first hand. He reached over and gave Dominique a stack.

Hand after hand, K-Dog was winning until the players left one at a time, leaving K-Dog and Dominique alone together.

"Hit my name is Kenny." K-Dog reached out his, she took it and at that moment, she felt something that she never felt experienced before.

"Wow!" was the only works to express what she was feeling.

"Umm… excuse me, Ms. Dominique, but are you okay?"

"Yeah, I'm alright, it just the energy you possessed with, it's breathtaking."

This was the first time in his life somebody ever told him that. Did this beautiful lady know something about him that he didn't know?

"I don't know what to say, but thanks."

She had him feeling like a kid again.

"You're welcome, Kenny."

Damn! The way she says my name, I wouldn't mind hearing it come from her mouth forever, K-Dog thought to his self.

It was obvious there was a connection between the two, K-Dog was feeling her, and Dominique was feeling him.

"I would like to get to know you a lil' better you know, what you like and what's your dislikes. I wanna get to know er'thang about you," K-Dog said, going in for the kill. Dominique took a while before responding.

"I think we can make it happen, it's strange because it's something about you that I would love to know." She couldn't believe she let that come out her mouth.

"I like the sound of that. I'll tell you what, how 'bout we exchange numbers and we can go from there."

"I got something better. I don't mean to come off too aggressive, but I get off work in ten minutes. How would you like to go get something to eat?" That alone put a smile on his face.

"That sounds like a plan. I'll meet you out front," K Dogg said, grabbing all his chips from off the table.

"Okay, I'll see you out front then."

K-Dog went to the window to exchange his winning chips in before heading towards the exit. Just as he was walking out, somebody bumped him with their shoulders without apologizing. "What the…" K-Dog caught himself while looking at a black male the same age as him. K-Dog thought he recognized him from somewhere, but he could not remember, so he decided to let it slide and turned, walking out of the door.

K-Dog was sitting in his Range Rover, playing R. Kelly when Dominique came out, strolling through the doors, looking like a goddess. Damn! She's beautiful, K-Dog thought to himself as he blew the horn, getting Dominique's attention.

Dominique walked towards K-Dog's S.U.V and opened the door and got in. Dominique had to admitted to herself that the brotha had class. "So, where would you like to go, Ms. Lady"? K-Dog asked as he was pulling off.

Dominique thought to herself before saying, "Honestly I don't know." Dominique batted her eyes before speaking again. "Do you have a place where we can eat?"

K-Dog looked over to her and smiled. "I know a place."

Evil Lurks
8:15 a.m.
Killa
CHAPTER 5

K illa was making moves in the game; he ran every spot in the hood. As for the workers he hired they were handling business like a dope spot should, and money was coming in like a freight train that it didn't make no sense.

Killa was getting ready to do a pickup and drop off at the trap like he always did every morning. But today something just didn't feel right as Killa sat on the edge of the king-sized bed, trying to get his thought process together when Precious asked, "Baby are you okay?"

"Yeah, bae, I'm good," Killa responded, getting up while walking inside their walk-in closet, putting on his bullet proof vest.

Precious watched Killa from the bed and she knew something wasn't right, so she got out of the bed and walked behind Killa, wrapping her arms around him.

"Killa, baby, please… baby, please, don't go. I feel something just isn't right," Precious said, begging him.

"Bae, everything is good, you don't have to worry,

okay?" Killa turned around and kissed Precious on her lips before walking out the front door. All Precious could do was say a prayer for Killa.

The fame, the money, even the house Killa bought for Precious, she hoped one day he'll marry her and start a family. Killa was thinking about his life and what the future held for him, and so much was going through his mind that he didn't notice he was being followed.

Just as Killa was pulling up in his Benz truck, at the red light on 19th and 27th Ave., a white bubble Chevy with tinted windows pulled up on the side of him and fired eight rounds.

Blocka! Blocka! Blocka! Blocka! Blocka! Blocka! Blocka!

Killa pulled off while reaching for his fye.

"Ahhh," Killa said, touching his left shoulder while, at the same time, gripping the steering wheel. Killa was hit but he had to think fast because the shooter was on his ass, busting shot after shot. Killa swerved into the other lane and started letting rounds go until the magazine was empty.

"Fuck!" Killa yelled to the top of his lungs, looking back at the shooter when out of the blue Killa lost control of his vehicle and crashed into a concrete pole, causing the vehicle to flip four times before landing upside down. Killa was unconscious until the police and paramedics came.

Within minutes, the scene had formed a very large crowd. Channel 7 News was on the scene with a live report by the reporter. People were calling on their cellphones, crying, telling people that somebody had killed Killa in broad daylight.

Killa's Benz truck was totally crushed on all sides and as for the roof, it was caved in. The firefighters had to cut the truck in half just for them to pull Killa free.

After K-Dog had received the news about Killa, he rushed to the scene. When he got there, K-Dog could not believe what he was seeing; the tragedy was a disaster. Precious was there crying her eyes out; she was totally losing her mind, K-Dog had to grab Precious to calm her down. K-Dog and Precious rode in the paramedics as they were escorting Killa to Broward General Hospital.

Seeking Revenge
Six Months Later
K-Dog
CHAPTER 6

Ever since Killa was put in the coma, K-Dog was really on guard. He had his team following him in unmarked vehicles just to be extra careful.

It was a $50,000 cash reward out for anybody with information pertaining to Killa's shooter; it was only a matter of time before somebody came forth. P r e c i o u s was pregnant with a baby girl and was on the verge of it having. K-Dog and Dominique had gotten engage, but the only thing was Killa.

Every other day, they all would get together, including Killa's mother, and they would go visit him like clock-work, even on Sundays Dominique and K-Dog attended church faithfully.

One early morning while K-Dog was laying in the bed next to Dominique, his cell phone started ranging.

"Hello."

"Umm… is this K-Dog?" the person on the other line asked.

"Yeah, dis him. Who wanna know?!" K-Dog didn't

recognize the voice or the number that displayed on his screen.

"Look, man, I'm just calling about da information pertaining to Killa's shooter." K-Dog sat straight up in his bed with his cell glued to his ear. Whoever the person was on the phone had his full undivided attention.

"I'm listenin', speak yo' mind." K-Dog looked over at Dominique who had her eyes fixed on him.

"I know who put da hit on Killa, but if I tell you how I know you'd give me da cash, and let alone let me live?"

"Because my word is my bond and my word are all I got," K-Dog said, letting the words sank in before continuing.

"Meet me at my warehouse on 27th across from da cemetery in thirty minutes. You think you could do dat?"

"Well, I don't know because how I'd know you won't put a bullet in my head?"

"As long as you come correct you have nothing to worry about." K-Dog hung up and got out the bed.

"Bae, somebody comin' forth with information about Killa's shooter," K-Dog said, walking where he had his stash at, pulling out $25,000.

"Finally, baby! That's good, but how do you know it's not a setup?" Dominique asked.

"Don't worry about dat, bae, you know yo man got dis." K-Dog walked up and planted a wet, sloppy kiss on Dominique's lips before walking out the front door.

Fifteen minutes later, K-Dog and his crew were standing out front at the warehouse, waiting for whoever was giving information about Killa's shooter.

K-Dog and his crew stood around, waiting, heavily armed with high/power assault rifles, and K-Dog even had snipers on the roof, giving him a bird's eye view, just in case shit got crazy.

Twenty minutes later, while K-Dog was standing out front, waiting, the sniper who was on the roof radioed the crew using a two way.

"It's a green B.M.W. pulling through da gates now... copy?"

"Copy dat," one of K-Dogs lieutenants responded into a hidden microphone that was attached to his wristed.

K-Dog stood in front of his crew as the S.U.V. pulled up and came to a complete halt. Seconds later, a slim light-skinned fellow exited and walked over to where K-Dog and his crew were, but before the fellow got within distances, K-Dog's L.T. stepped up, stopping him and patted him down thoroughly.

"He's clean," the lieutenant said.

K-Dog waved him over for him to approach, and when he did, K-Dog looked him dead in the eyes like he was looking through his soul.

"Give me what I want," was the only thing K-Dog said. The guy looked around and saw all the armed men standing around. He swallowed and thought about what he was gonna say, choosing his words wisely.

"My name is Mike, and I use to roll with Pimp back in days when he was on his shit. Well, not too long ago, I attendant a party and Pimp was there with a couple of his partners. I walked over and greeted him outta respect, and that's when I overheard his conversation, and he was talking about how he wished his boys ran down on Killa and how he wished it was you instead of Killa." The fellow looked around before continuing. "I waited until I made sure what I was hearing was facts, because I didn't wanna give you the wrong info, knowing my life depends on it." Now this was what K-Dog been waiting for, finally, it came to the light.

"You 100% sure what you are telling me is true because if you lyin? I promise you; I'd find you and kill you and yo' family… do I make myself clear?!" K-Dog got in the guy's face to let him feel what he was saying.

"I understand… as a matter of fact, I've written down every address to my family, just to show you what I'm tellin' you is da truth." The guy reached into his pockets and handed K-Dog a piece of paper. K-Dog accepted the piece of paper.

"Okay, my friend. I appreciate dis." K-Dog walked over to his vehicle and grabbed a brown paper bag and gave it to him.

"Dis $25,000 up front, I'll give you da rest after I take care of Pimp, you have my word on dat." The fellow took the bag and got back into his vehicle and pulled off. K-Dog turned to his L.T. and said.

"Follow him and report every move he makes; I waited a long time for dis. Find Pimp's whereabouts and let me know," with that being said, K-Dog jumped into his Range Rover and pulled off.

***

Two Weeks Later…

Always be prepared for the unexpected the element of surprise is a muhfucka, an enemy will lay and wait for the perfect time to strike. K-Dog had to plan his way through this, because at this moment, time were crucial, and one false move you could get checked.

It wasn't long before K-Dog found out Pimp's whereabouts after receiving the information, and K-Dog was going in for the kill. K-Dog had his Take Over to stalk out where Pimp was for two days after they got word where Pimp was located.

It was a Monday night, 11:45 p.m. and who would've

known that death was waiting around the corner. K-Dog and his team of killers was in position, getting ready to kick in the apartment door where Pimp was. The complex's apartment where Pimp was at were located off Broward and Powerline. K-Dog had the entire complex surrounded, nobody was able to enter or exit.

The apartment where Pimp was at was downstairs, and K-Dog put his ear to door, listening closely. The only thing that could've been heard was the television. Without any hesitation, K-Dog stood back with his pistol in hand and counted to three.

Boom! One of K-Dog's henchman kicked the door off the hinges before running in, upping choppas. Once everybody was seized, K-Dog walked in, wearing all/black with his throw away—unclean gun—in his hand and walked where Pimp and his two partners were. When Pimp laid eyes on K-Dog, he already knew he was a dead man. Pimp put his head down and said a silent prayer.

"Pimp, my man, wuz up with you? It's been a long time since we last seen each other," K-Dog said, snatching the duct tape from off Pimps mouth.

"You know why I'm here right?" K-Dog pulled up a chair and sat in front of Pimp.

"Of course you do, shame on you, my friend because tonight, is going to be just for you to make a wish before you go to see the creator..." K-Dog was cut off by Pimp as he busted out laughing right in K-Dog's face.

"Listen, lil' nigga let's get one thing straight tonight..." Pimp said, looking death K-Dog dead in the eyes. "Regardless if you kill me or not, it doesn't matter, because I played my part in dis world. And the only thing that's promised to us is death. So, however, I can accept my fate, I just hope you could accept it when it comes around for you. Because believe it or not your time comin'." K-Dog stood up and pointed his throw away at Pimp's face.

"You know, Pimp. I was responsible for killing yo' wife and takin yo' $1.5 mill, dats right, it was me. Everything you once owned belongs to me." K-Dog pulled the hammer back.

Click!

"Until the time comes when it's my turn to meet my maker, make sure you tell yo' wife I said, hello," K-Dog said, pulling the trigger and blowing the back of Pimp's skull out, knocking his brains on the wall. Just as K-Dog was walking out the apartment two more shots was fired; all head shots, leaving behind a pool of blood.

***

"Damn, Killa, man, I pray you pull thru dis shit, don't do dis to me... I need man," K-Dog said to himself as he was sitting inside his vehicle, parked out front of his residence. K-Dog's head was spinning a 100 m.p.h. as he thought about Killa's situation.

Pimp was no longer breathing, and even though Pimp was dead, it couldn't make Killa's situation no better than it was.

Finally, after clearing his mind, K-Dog got his thoughts together as he exited his Range Rover, looking at the time: 2:47 a.m. K-Dog had no idea that Dominique was sitting in the front room, until he came strolling through the front door, and there she was rushing in his direction with open arms, greeting her king.

"Hey, baby. I'm glad you home. I was worried about you," Dominique said while embracing K-Dog as she laid, she her head in the center of his chest. K-Dog stroked Dominique's head with gentle touches running his fingers through her hair.

"I'm good, sweetheart, ain't no need to be worrying baby." K-Dog looked into his future wife's eyes, knowing it would tear Dominique's heart in half if something ever happened to him. Just the thought alone made K-Dog embrace Dominique more.

"I ain't neva going nowhere, and I want you to understand that okay." K-Dog swept Dominique off her feet and walked into their bedroom, closing the door behind them.

K-Dog was in the shower, standing under the warm water, letting it run over his body, as he thought about Pimps words, replaying over and repeatedly. "I played my part in this world, and the only thing promised to us is death. I just hope you can accept it when it comes around for you because believe it or not your time coming."

It's funny how the game has its twist and turns. As a youth, you really have no worries, but all that innocent shit is gone out of the window. K-Dog is in the big leagues and in too deep, living by the codes of the streets... you live by the gun, you die by the gun.

Finally, getting outta of the shower, K-Dog walked into their master bedroom, wearing a pair of boxers, K-Dog noticed Dominique watching him as he was lotion his body. By the look of it, Dominique had something to say, so she crawled towards K-Dog, sitting on the edge of the bed and started rubbing his back. "Baby, I have been thinking a lot about you," Dominique said as she massaged K-Dog's back.

"Me? About what?"

"Everything silly," Dominique responded while hitting him playfully on the arm.

"Kenny, listen boy, okay?" Dominique got up and stood in front of K-Dog looking him in his eyes.

"I love you, boy, dearly with all of my being, sweetie, and the life you live and what not, I understand it. I really do, but have you ever thought about making a transformation? You know letting go of all the street stuff, everything that's negative and turn it around … you know into something positive?"

K-Dog thought about what Dominique just said pertaining to his lifestyle which he lived all his life. As a victim of circumstances, K-Dog was a product of his inhabitants.

Dominique knew that the wheels was turning into his head, so she pressed on.

"Sweetie, I believe in you, but you got to believe in yourself." Dominique reached out, caressing the side of K-Dog's face with the softness of her fingertips.

"Do you even know the power and energy that you possess, the influence and impact you have over the communities? It's a gift given from God. The reason, I'm telling you this is because I see something in you that you don't see in yourself. Do you know what I seen and why I fell in love with you, the very first time, I laid eyes on you?"

K-Dog thought it before asking. "What?"

"Greatness! I see a man that has great potentials to be the very best, all he has to do is be willing to make a change. You can be so much more then you are today… my love search deep within yourself, and I promise you will find who you are truly made to be." Dominique had tears falling from her eyes as she expressed her love for him.

K-Dog listened to Dominique's every word because it made a whole lotta sense. You know the saying... It takes a real woman to bring the best out of a man.

Life or Death
Killa
CHAPTER 7

There was a tunnel, and inside of this tunnel was a very bright light. Killa was standing in the middle of the tunnel. People who Killa knew like family, friends, and loved ones were calling Killa to turn around and come back, but on the other side of the tunnel, was something pulling him deeper and deeper into tunnel. It was a face glowing like the sun at the other end of the tunnel and had the form of an angel. Whatever it was, was making Killa walk towards it, but on the other side of the tunnel, were screams from everybody.

Finally, Killa turned around when he heard the voice of Precious, telling him to stop and come back. Her stomach was big and round, and Precious rubbed her belly while reaching out her hand with tears in her eyes.

A voice told Killa from inside the bright tunnel, if he wanted to live and see his family again, he had to fight to resist the force that was pulling him, or let the force swallow him in. For a minute, Killa looked from side to side, from one end to another, he had to make a choice, give up or fight. Killa decided to fight against the force that was pulling him in. Killa reached out his hands towards Precious and started walking in her direction.

"Nooooo!" the force said while changing from different images every second. Killa started running, using all his strength he had to resist the force, he ran and ran until he reached Precious and his family. At that very moment, Killa's eyes opened and closed, but his vision was blurry. He had to open and close his eyes until his vision became clear. The nurse had just walked into the room, when she noticed slight movements were coming from Killa, she rushed to Killa's side.

"Sir, can you hear me?" the nurse said, grabbing Killa's hand. But Killa's hand just looked at her, trying to figure out where he was.

"If you can hear me, squeeze my hand for me." Killa squeezed the nurse hand.

"Good... it's good to have you back."

Hours later, Killa's room was filled with family and friends; everybody came to show they're support. They bought balloons and gifts and gave them to him; the doctor couldn't believe what he was seeing. Killa was up, talking and laughing like nothing happen, they never seen something like this... never!

Precious was by Killa's side, looking like she was pregnant with twins. She was glad to see her man back to himself, but most of all, Precious was glad Killa was alive. After everybody left the room, leaving Killa and K-Dog alone, it was time for K-Dog to inform Killa on the situation pertaining to Pimp.

"I'm glad you pulled through, soulja," K-Dog said, putting his hand on Killa's shoulder.

"Yeah, man, me too," Killa said as he stuffed his mouth with the food Precious and the rest of them bought for him. Killa was eating like he hadn't eaten in years;

varieties of food were scattered across Killa's bed as he ate from them.

"Bruh, you won't believe who was responsible for doin dis to you."

"Who?!" Killa said, looking K-Dog straight in the eyes.

"It was Pimp."

"You for real, nigga?!" Killa flipped the plates of food off his bed.

"I swear to God, I'ma kill dat nigga and whoever had sum'thin to do with it." Killa was trying to get out his hospital bed.

"Calm down, my boy, you don't have to worry. I've already took care of the job," K-Dog said.

"So, you mean…"

"He's dead as a doorknob," K-Dog said as a matter of fact, cutting Killa off midsentence. K-Dog knew how Killa was feeling about the whole situation, Killa been in a coma for eight long months.

"Look, nigga, forget about dat shit. Da only thing dat matters is you're alive. Now get in gear and get on ya feet soulja!" K-Dog yelled while walking over to the chair that had Killa's clothes sitting on it.

K-Dog reached into the bag grabbing the items inside, giving them to Killa to put on.

Minutes later, Killa was fully dressed, rocking a polo outfit, when out the blue Precious walked inside with Killa's mother. She was doing a lot better with the help of K-Dog. Ms. Vanessa was no longer doing drugs at all, her weight had picked up, and when Killa saw her all he could do was smile.

***

Three Weeks Later...

Killa was back on his feet, up and running like nothing ever happened to him. The whole time while Killa was home, Precious took care of him, despite of her pregnancy which was do less than a week.

On the behalf of Killa, he was a very blessed young man. Just weeks ago, he was in a coma for eight months, and to be alive after being shot twice, it was nothing but the power of God.

Killa was riding in his brand-new Porsche truck, cruising up Broward Blvd and 441, when an old lady was walking up the street, carrying grocery bags. From the looks of it, the old lady was having trouble carrying her bags and needed help, Killa pulled over, got out his vehicle, and waited for her.

"How you doin', ma'am?" Killa said to the old lady. She stopped and looked at Killa before responding.

"I'm blessed, young man, just trying to make my way home," the old woman said, placing the grocery bags on the pavement.

"That's the reason why I pulled over because you looked like you needed help."

"Aww... bless your heart," the old woman said as Killa opened the passenger door.

"I'm only here to help, ma'am." The old woman saw the compassionate look in Killa's eyes and wasted no time getting in. Killa closed the door, grabbing the bags before pulling them into the back seat of his Porsche truck S.U.V. Killa walked towards the driver door after closing the back door, opening it, and getting in.

Seconds later, Killa pulled off, heading west on Broward Blvd, the elder asked.

"What is your name, young fellow?"

"Keith, ma'am... Keith Thomas," Killa responded, knowing she was observing him closely as he was driving.

"Which street do you live on?" Killa asked.

"Make a right on 3rd street and go all the way down towards the dead-end, Keith," the elder said, pointing in the direction she wanted Killa to go.

"I must say, young man, this here is a mighty fine vehicle. It's expensive. To be honest with you, this is the very first-time riding in something like this," the elder said while running her hands over the leather interior.

"What do you call this truck, sweetie? I see the name, but my eyes are bad, and I don't have on my reading glasses."

"It's a Porsche S.U.V., ma'am," Killa responded as he was pulling in some condominium called Green Village.

"Pull right in and park right next to this blue vehicle." Killa pulled in and parked.

"Well, thank you so much, sugar. I'm very thankful" the elder woman said, opening the door. Before she was able to exit Killa's vehicle, a light-skinned slim girl walked up.

"Grandma, who is this giving you a ride?" the female said, looking in Killa's direction.

"Oh, baby, this is Keith, and all he was doing was giving me a ride," the elder said as she was exiting Killa's vehicle.

"Grandma, you know you shouldn't be catching a ride with no stranger; people are crazy out here these days."

"I know, sugar, but this one right here is special," the elder told her granddaughter.

Killa got out of his vehicle and opened the back door grabbing the elderly woman grocery bags and gave them to the girl.

"This one is special," the elder said noticing how her granddaughter was looking at Killa.

"Take care, sweetie," she said, walking off, leaving the two alone.

"Excuse me, ma'am!" Killa yelled out stopping her in her tracks.

"Yes."

"What's yo' name?"

"Mrs. Roberts... Willie Mae Roberts," she responded while turning back around and walking off.

"Hi, my name is Sharon, but everybody calls me Bray."

"It's nice to meet you, Bray." Killa extended his hand-out.

"The same here," Bray responded while accepting Killa's token.

Just by Killa's appearance, Bray knew Killa was a heavy hitter. His clothes, jewels, even his vehicle was top of the line.

Special ah... Bray thought to herself.

"Thank you once again for giving my grandmother a ride."

"No problem," Killa said, smiling to his self, showing his iced-out grill.

"What!" Bray said, noticing Killa was smiling at her.

"Nothing... I was just thinking how you and yo. grandmother look so much alike."

"You kidding me, right? Because this is the first time anybody mention that about us," Bray said, shaking her head.

"It's a first time for everything, Bray." She smiled and not even aware she was smiling.

"Well, take care of yourself." Killa walked back around towards the driver side of his vehicle, Killa got in, rolling the passenger window down.

"Make sure you look out for, Mrs. Roberts."

"I will," with that be said Killa pulled off.

***

Killa had just pulled up on the block in the hood, and nothing had changed but a few faces, everything else was still the same. One of Killa's young workers who name was Lil' Coon walked up on Killa as he was exiting his S.U.V.

"Lil' Coon, wat are you doing with da money you making out here?" Killa asked.

"Putting every dollar away like you told me," Lil' Coon responded.

One of the reasons why Killa took a liking to Lil' Coon in the first place was because he reminded him so much of himself. Young, ambition, and fearless! Every chance Killa got, he stayed dropping jewels on the youngster.

The two chopped it up for a while as they watched the hustlers and the fiends interact with one another. 7th CT was always on fire 24/7 in the hood, because 7th CT was a million-dollar street. In the hood, if you had a million-dollar street where niggaz could get rich, just off slanging rocks, then that's the street where all the action goes down.

After eight months in the coma, Lil' Coon was still going hard on the block, he even remained loyal. Killa knew Lil' Coon was street certified the very first time he laid eyes on him, and that's why he decided to put Lil' Coon on. But today Killa gave Lil' Coon the position to be his L.T. and his right-hand man.

CHAPTER 8

K-Dog was getting ready to hit the surprise party he planned for Killa tonight. Everybody was already there, waiting for K-Dog and Killa to come through. B.G., Killa's favorite rapper, was there along with Young Jeezy, Lil' Boosie, and Webbie, and not to mention a lot of bad ass strippers. Tonight, K-Dog wanted this night to be for Killa, so he went out of his way to make this night special for Killa.

K-Dog was walking out his front door, calling Killa and telling him to be ready in twenty minutes because he was on his way. K-Dog never told Killa where he was going tonight, all K-Dog told Killa was to dress nice and not to worry, he was in good hands.

Twenty minutes later, K-Dog was pulling up in front of Killa's crib, blowing the horn. Before K-Dog was able to put his Range Rover in park good enough, Killa came walking out in an all-white linen suit with the hard bottom shoe to match.

Killa was striving towards K-Dog's S.U.V. smooth like he was walking on a cloud. K-Dog noticed a slight change in Killa ever since he pulled through out of the coma. Killa started rocking white more frequently on a day-to-day basis, and every time you saw him, it looked like he was skating instead of walking.

Finally, walking to the S.U.V., Killa opened the door and get in. He gave K-Dog a firm handshake before readjusting his fire that was concealed on his waistline.

"Wuz gud with you, dawg?" Killa said as K-Dog was pulling off.

"You already know, anotha day, anotha dollar… Killa let me ask you sum'thin."

"Wuz up, bruh?" Killa said, looking over at K-Dog.

"Ever since you came out the coma, bruh, why you started rockin white?"

"Because, bruh, I'm pure now and besides white symbolize purity," Killa said, smiling to his self.

"And where we going, bruh?" K-Dog didn't respond, he just looked over at Killa and smiled as he continued driving.

Twenty minutes later, K-Dog pulled in the Marriot, parking next to a bunch of limousines, that was located on Fort Lauderdale Beach. All types of foreign vehicles sitting on big boy tires, were parked throughout the parking lot, that it looked more like a car show. Killa was looking around like 'why we are pulling up to a Hotel?' Little did he know tonight would be the night that will always be in his memory.

Moment later, they both exited the vehicle, walking into the hotel.

"Dis way, bruh," K-Dog said, walking up to the elevator, pushing the button.

Ding!

The door opened and they both got off on the top floor, known as the penthouse. K-Dog pulled out a plastic card and inserted it into the card hole, unlocking the door.

When K-Dog opened the door, the room was dark.

"Killa, go to the wall and turn the lights on," K-Dog told him while closing the door. Killa walked over, switching the lights on, and soon they came on and everybody yelled to the top of their lungs.

"Surprise!" Killa stood there shocked, looking at every face.

"What da fuck," Killa said to himself, looking at the face of his favorite rappers.

"Dis surprise party goes out to you, homie. I couldn't done dis alone, so look around and see you got da whole Take Over family present, they help me put dis thing together bruh." K-Dog walked up to Killa, placing his arm around his neck.

"I hope you enjoy it more than I enjoyed putting it together. I put dis together with the rest of the team, to show you how much we care about you, Killa. Now let's enjoy ourselves like never before. I dedicate dis to you, bruh." K-Dog walked out, leaving Killa to do his thang.

***

Killa mainly chilled out with B.G., vibing while smoking the best loud money could buy. The entire room was filled with major playas, big money on top of money was on deck, and money was flying all over the place, falling on the strippers as they did their thing.

K-Dog was amongst the rappers, shooting dice with a black bottle of liquor in his hands, talking cash shit. Lil' Boosie and Young Jeezy couldn't believe how K-Dog was pointing with the dice; he was winning all their money.

Killa really didn't pay too much of attention to the strippers as they walked around naked, until he laid eyes on this bad one. Baby was flawless and had a body like a goddess; she was just that fine.

K-Dog noticed he kept making eye contact with this particular dude who was at the party, and not only that, but the same dude was watching Killa too close, and that made K-Dog throw up a red flag. K-Dog decided to go the balcony where he could watch the dude more closely. As K-Dog past dude, he stared K-Dog down like he had a problem and that seemed real strange. When K-Dog reached the balcony, he placed his back against the rail and observed this cat through the glass sliding door. Something about him made K-Dog feel uncomfortable for some reason, and the way he was staring Killa down, K-Dog knew that look… it was pure evil.

For twenty minutes, K-Dog observed the cat until he couldn't take it any longer. He walked back inside and approached one of his henchmen who was getting a lap dance by one of the strippers.

"Check me out, bruh, right quick," K-Dog said while walking into the hallway. Seconds later, the henchman stepped into the hallway, closing the door behind him.

"Wuz up, boss?" he said, walking up to K-Dog. "You look like something on yo mind."

K-Dog didn't respond as he leaned back on the wall, thinking to himself for a couple seconds, before saying.

"Dat dude dats standing in the corner, is making me feel uneasy."

"Why you stay dat, boss?"

"Because all night dis nigga been doing is staring me and Killa down like he got pressure… you know I dat instinct." K-Dog rubbed his chin.

"Well, wat you won't me to do… kill da nigga? Give me da word."

"Just sit back and watch his every move, I wanna know who he is, and I wanna know er'thang about dis nigga."

"Say no more, boss; I got dis," K-Dog's henchman said.

K-Dog walked back inside the hotel room with his henchman right behind him, instead of joining the party, K-Dog went back out on the balcony only to find a stripper out there, smoking a blunt. K-Dog paid her no attention as he walked towards the rail, putting both arms on top of it while looking towards the ocean.

K-Dog didn't know the stripper was watching him, but she could tell a lot was on his mind. This was the King of the city that was standing next to her, and she wanted to do something special for him, so she walked up placing her hand on his shoulder and saying, "Daddy you look like you got a lot of shit on yo mind." K-Dog took a deep breath, trying to relax a little before turning around and facing her.

"Naw, I'm straight, ma, just tryna think things over a lil bit… dats all."

"Oh, really?" she said, stepping closer to him placing her hand on his dick. She unzipped K-Dog's designer pants while reaching into them pulling out his dick. Before K-Dog had time to do anything, she slipped him in the warmest of her mouth and stared sucking him off real nice.

Everything K-Dog was thinking about had went out the window, she was sucking him sooo good, the only thing K-Dog could focus on was how this beautiful creature was pleasing him. Her head game was vicious. While she was sucking him off, she was using both of her hands, jacking and massaging his dick. Less than five minutes, K-Dog busted in her mouth.

With that said and done, the stripper grabbed her things and went back inside to join the party, leaving K-Dog out there by himself… mission accomplish.

Game On
K-Dog
CHAPTER 9

It's been a whole week since the party K-Dog had thrown for Killa, but for Killa it seems like it was just yesterday. He was still doing his "1-2" in the streets, distributing large amount of cocaine, but the only difference is now was that Killa was cautious.

Precious had just birth they're baby girl less than a week ago, and they both agreed to name her Rayanna. Every chance Killa got, he was showering her with the finest things money could buy, money wasn't a thing because the game had been good to him. All Killa wanted was for his family to be happy.

The lifestyle Killa was living was good, but he wanted so much outta life then what it was offering. Killa wanted to be somebody and not just a dope boy. He had a family to support, which was his responsibility, hands down. But knowing the life he lived, it wasn't always peaches and cream.

Killa was home in his bed, holding his baby girl, while lying next to Precious, when his cell phone went off.

"Hello," Killa answered it on the third ring.

"Killa, wuz gud?"

"Ay, boy, I got sum news for you too, bruh, on sum real nigga shit." By the sound of K-Dog's voice, Killa knew it was serious.

"Bruh, meet me at da spot in twenty minutes."

"Aight," Killa responded.

"Bruh, dis is sum deep shit, so strap up."

"I got cha." Killa ended the call, laying little Rayanna next to Precious. He got up and walked towards the closet, grabbing his bullet proof vest. Precious was looking at Killa with that look, because this very scene took her back eight months ago when Killa was shot, let alone put in a coma. Killa knew Precious was watching his every move and he knew where her mind was at, so Killa sat next to her.

"Wuz wrong, boo?" Killa said.

"Keith, don't do dis to me again... please, baby. I don't know what I'll do if something happens to you." Precious had tears forming in her eyes.

"Baby, listen... you don't have to worry about sum'thin like that ever as long as I'm in good strength and good health. I will neva leave y'all side; I promise." Killa wiped the tears that was coming from Precious eyes before kissing her and Rayanna.

"I love you, Keith."

"I love you too, baby." Killa said, getting up, walking out the door.

Twenty minutes later, Killa was pulling up at one of their spots, off 31st and 2nd street. K-Dog and the crew were waiting for Killa to come at the spot; they all dressed in all black, carrying assault rifles.

When Killa pulled up and exited his vehicle, he already knew the situation at hand was a serious matter. Killa walked up to K-Dog and the members that were standing out front shook their hands before entering the house.

They all sat at the table, taking their positions, K-Dog was sitting at the head of the table, smoking a Cuban cigar. Killa was sitting on the right side of K-Dog while the other members followed suit. Once everybody was sitting in the rightfully position, K-Dog looked at every one of them, making sure they were focused before speaking. "Now that everyone is here, I want you all to understand, that we are dealing with a serious problem…" K-Dog stopped only for a brief moment to make sure he had everybody's attention before continuing. "Dis problem at hand needs to be taken care of immediately, no question asked. Why? Because it's bad for business and for us." K-Dog looked directly at Killa, letting him know that the situation was about both of them. "Killa, you remember a while back when we were kids at the park, and you beat da hell out that one kid?" Killa was trying to remember what kid K-Dog was referring to.

"Bruh, I beat da hell outta a lot of niggas. Which one are you talking about?" Everybody stated laughing, including Killa.

"Nigga, I'm talking about da kid at the park you beat down, around the time when we were dealing with what's his name…"

"Pimp," Killa responded, finishing K-Dog sentence.

"Now you are getting it."

"I remember that, but I can't recall his name. Let alone, I wouldn't recognize da cat if I saw his face."

"That's the dangerous part Killa, recognizing who dis individual is."

"I don't understand, bruh, dis shit been damn near ten years ago. Why it's so important to recognize dis cat? What he got to do with any of dis?" Killa said looking confused.

"Well… to bring it to yo' attention, that same individual who you beat down that day, let's just say he's back for revenge," K-Dog said, blowing smoke from the Cuban Cigar.

"Revenge!" Killa stood up, placing his hands on the table while looking over at K-Dog.

"Yes, Killa, revenge." K-Dog sat back in his chair, knowing Killa didn't have any idea that this cat was responsible for putting him in the coma. K-Dog decided to put Killa on point about the whole situation at hand, so he leaned forward in his chair with the Cuban placed in the corner of his mouth.

"For some reason, dis cat is tryna bring what we built to da ground, and I think, or should I say I know, he's responsible for putting you in a coma." Killa eyes got big like to golf balls, that got his attention.

What! Can you image what was going through Killa's mind, murdering this nigga was the only thing going through his head. K-Dog knew what Killa was thinking, he saw it in his eyes.

"You remember da party; I threw for you?" K-Dog asked.

"Yeah, man, how could I forget."

"I don't know if you noticed it or not, but while we were celebrating, it was on person sticking out like a sore thumb. I noticed he was watching you like a hawk, watching his prey; da vibe he was giving me wasn't right. So, I had one of our members find all dat he could about dude, and I got what I wanted." K-Dog picked up a folder from off the floor and passed it to Killa. Killa opened it and examined what was inside.

"Dis that same car that pulled on da side of me and open fire," Killa said as he flipped through the pictures one at a time for about two minutes, before putting them down on the table. Killa looked at the ceiling before saying.

"Yeah, I remember seeing him at da party…" Killa paused, tryna control the anger that was building up inside of him.

"I waited a long time to put a bullet in dis nigga head."

"I know dawg, and I understand how you feeling, and whatever you got on yo' mind you know I'm down by law, and da rest of da team is. Wuz on yo' mind bruh?"

Killa looked into K-Dogs' eyes and said, "Murder."

Retaliation
K-Dog
CHAPTER 10

K-Dog was lying next to Dominique in the bed, thinking about how they were gonna run down on buddy tonight. This whole thing about buddy situation was throwing K-Dog into a loop, but one thing was fo-sho, whatever buddy had on his chest it was time to get put on his ass. Everything was going fine in K-Dog's life. He met a very beautiful girl that he plans on spending the rest of his life with, his car lot business was doing numbers, and money was coming like a freight train. The empire he built from the ground up came from the five qualities which were principles he lived by: Will, Determination, Focus, Discipline, and Sacrifice were K-Dogs foundation which he stood on.

The whole day, K-Dog chilled home like he promised Dominique he would. They watched movies, ate pizza, and had ice cream; they even did the boyfriend and girlfriend thing.

Even though there was unfinished business that had to be dealt with, like chess, K-Dog knew his opponents every move. So, he decided to make a call just to see if everything was 54, K-Dog picked up his cell and called his eyes.

"Yeah, boss."

"Wuz da 4-1-1?" K-Dog asked while looking over at Dominique.

"I'm still parked out front, watching dis nigga get his dick sucked inside sum hood rat house."

"Okay, dats good, because after tonight, he will be his last time busting a nut," K-Dog said in a low but harsh voice.

"Keep yom eyes and yo' ears open, soulja."

"Aight, boss; I got cha." K-Dog ended the call.

"Baby, whose last time busting a nut?" Dominique asked.

"Nobody, girl. Now come here!" K-Dog grabbed Dominique, pulling her on top of him; it was time for him to put in work.

Around 12:46 a.m. it was time for K-Dog to put his plan into play. Killa was outside, waiting on him, so they could run down on fooly. This was the perfect time to catch him, because he was slipping with his pants down, or so they thought, and that's how K-Dog and Killa wanted to leave him... with his dick in the dirt.

K-Dog knew in order for him to go anywhere, without having to explain his whereabouts to Dominique, then he had to give her a shot of her medicine... good sex! Just as K-Dog was walking out the door, he checked his fi, making sure his bullet proof vest was in place before he walked out the door. As K-Dog was walking towards the vehicle, he noticed the expression that was displaced across Killa's face... murder!

Finally, reaching the vehicle K-Dog opened the front passenger door and got in. When he closed the door, Killa pulled off without saying a word. K-Dog knew Killa was in deep thought; he had a lot on his mind. So, while Killa drove, K-Dog didn't say a word outta respect until Killa finally broke the silence.

"I'ma kill dis nigga, and everybody else who's with him so help me God." K-Dog just looked over at his boy. They had been down since day one like real brothas. K-Dog wanted the dude dead more than Killa.

"I feel you, dawg," K-Dog said, concealing his anger. He was good at it, let alone concealing his attention, and that's what made him very dangerous.

Killa was expressing his feelings the whole ride until they pulled up a couple houses down from where their target was located, and parked right behind one of their members, who was already there keeping an eye out on dude. Once Killa parked, he waited for the member to approach, and let the driver side window down.

"It's just him and da girl in there," the member said as he stuck his head into the window. Killa and K-Dog could've easily paid one of their henchmen to take care of the problem, but this one was personal, and they had to do it themselves.

As the three were getting ready to make their move on the target, out the blue the front door flew open and a male figure stepped out with an AK-47, and he started firing in their direction.

Killa and K-Dog was caught between a rock in a hard place. But being that they were swift on their toes, they easily maneuvered, jumping behind the vehicle and returning fire.

The three of them couldn't believe what they were seeing, they had got caught slippin'. Bullets were piercing the vehicle, knocking out chunks at a time, and the wind shield was no longer in place; it was shattered glass in the front seat.

"Pete! I thought you had everything covered," K-Dog said, while taking his fye out from his waistband and letting rounds loose. Killa and Pete followed suit also and started busting rounds as well.

"Shit! He still coming," Killa said, sticking his head out from behind the car.

"Look, we can't stay behind this car too long. We gotta split up, make it difficult for him." There was a line of vehicles on both sides of the road. At that moment, the lightbulb went off inside Killa's head.

"I'ma run cross the street while you guys cover for me," Killa said.

"1, 2, 3." K-Dog and Pete got up and started letting go round after round while Killa ran cross the street, getting on the other side of the vehicles, facing the sidewalk.

This dude that was shooting at them turned out to be the target. He must've had a 100-round clip by how he kept firing. He stayed low as he worked his way closer from car to car, trying to get a clear shot. The target had no idea that Killa was on the other side of the street as he advanced, inchin' closer and closer. The target was three cars away from K-Dog and Pete who ran out of bullets.

As the target stepped out from in front of a vehicle, making his way towards the next one, pining K-Dog and Pete down, Killa pointed in the shooter direction, squeezing the trigger.

Boom! Boom!

Both bullets penetrated, hitting him in the torso, knocking him right off his feet.

Killa didn't waste anytime as he ran up and stood over the target, blood was oozing everywhere. K-Dog and Pete also ran up, kicking the gun out of his reach.

"Make sure y'all watch him," Killa said before running towards the house. Killa entered the house with his fi out, moments later, shots rang out and he didn't say a word, and without any hesitation, he pointed the gun at the target's head, and emptied the rest of the clip into his head, killing him execution style, leaving his body restless.

Precious was asleep with Rayanna in the bed when he walked inside the bedroom, and all he could do was look at the two while they slept, thinking to himself. Nothing would never take him from them... was going through Killa's mind as he stood, leaning on the room door.

Precious must've felt Killa's presence because she opened her eyes.

"Baby, is dat you?" Precious said, rubbing her eyes.

"Yeah, it's me." Killa walked towards the edge of the bed and sat down.

"Is everything okay with you honey?" Precious said, sitting up, but not trying to wake up Rayanna.

"Everythin' good, ma. I'm just fena take a shower right quick. Go back to bed love, okay." Killa got up and kissed Precious on her lips before grabbing a pair of boxers. Killa walked into the bathroom, turning the water on warm. Seconds later, he stripped down and jumped head-first into the shower, letting the water run over his body.

For some odd reason, the scene that took place hours ago was playing in his head over and over again. Not only did Killa kill his enemy execution style, but the female who was inside the house, Killa took her out also, leaving her dead for her family to see. But the most important thing was his enemy was no longer walking around on God's green earth. And as for homegirl, she was in the wrong place at the wrong time... that's just how the game goes... may God rest her soul.

For Better or Worst
K-Dog
CHAPTER 11

K-Dog was sitting at his desk, in his office at the car lot thinking about what Dominique said about him getting out the game. Even though if K-Dog decided to get out the game and change his life around, it isn't that easy, especially not for him. K-Dog was still young and at his prime of his life; he was rich. A lot of niggas who enter the game never made it to where he was at, they only wished to walk in his shoes... and for that very reason, they envied him.

Something had to give because the lifestyle K-Dog was living, only led to two things: death or the penitentiary. Dominique gave K-Dog a deadline to make his decision, and that's what he was pondering on as he sat inside his office.

K-Dog loved Dominique dearly and would do anything to make her happy... God knowns he would. But the lifestyle that K-Dog lived was like second nature to him, and for him to just give it all up for the sake of love... Damn! That's the hardest thing for him to do. The street life was all that he knew, and for him to turn from it was difficult than K-Dog expected, not because he wanted more fame or more money, but because he was afraid of not knowing what the future held for him if he let it go. But regardless he knew today he had to face his fears or give up something that only comes once in a lifetime... Dominique.

Later that day, after K-Dog closed the car lot and made a few errands, he was pulling up at his residence and sat inside of his vehicle. K-Dog was contemplating what and how he was going to explain his situation about his lifestyle to Dominique; this was thus far the hardest thing for him to do.

K-Dog allowed his thoughts to run along with his true feelings until he felt he was ready to face up. Ain't no turning back, K-Dog said to himself as he exited his Range Rover.

The moment K-Dog walked through the front door, he knew by the smell of it, Dominique were throwing down in the kitchen.

"Baby, is that's you?" Dominique yelled as she walked out the kitchen, wearing absolutely nothing, exposing the perfectly body of a Goddess. K-Dog never saw her cooking dinner before naked, so this had to be something special for him, or could this be the last time he would ever see Dominique's body again if he refused to give the game up. Or could Dominique be his's forever, if only K-Dog decided to live a normal life.

This was going through K-Dogs head as he looked at what he craved forever since he laid eyes on her.

"What's wrong with you, baby? You look like you never saw me naked before?" Dominique said as she ran her hands over the curves of her body. K-Dog cleared his mind as he walked up, embracing her with a hug.

"Naw, boo, I was just admiring how beautiful you

are."

"Well, thanks, because you don't look to bad your-self." Dominique stepped back to look at him. "I got a surprise for you." Dominique grabbed K-Dog by the hand and led him into the kitchen.

"And wat do we have here, Ms. Lady?" K-Dog asked as he looked over the food Dominique prepared.

"Lobster, shrimp, and corn on the cob."

"Now dats wat I'm talking 'bout." K-Dog reached over and grabbed her butt. "And wuz for dessert?"

"Well, let's see, that's depends on you, my dear," Dominique responded.

"Oh, so it's like dat?"

"Yep! Just like that. Now take your seat, so we can eat."

K-Dog sat down like she said and watched her do her thing. Dominique fixed their plates, and also poured a glass of wine for them both.

The whole time they were eating, K-Dog was lusting for her in a major way, but Dominique had some news for him that would change their lives forever. The only problem was, how she was going tell K-Dog she was pregnant with his child. All types of 'what if?' possibilities were going through Dominique's head. What if K-Dog decided to continue running the streets? What if K-Dog wouldn't accept the seed that he planted? These were the thoughts that kept playing in her head.

After Dominique and K-Dog finished eating, they decided to take it to their bedroom. The whole time while Dominique was leading the way K-Dog was lost as he watched her back side; baby was walking like she was an American next top model. Once they entered their bedroom, Dominique got into the bed while K-Dog stood, slowly spreading her legs for K-Dog to see her pretty, shaved pink pussy. K-Dog tried to climb on top of Dominique, but she pushed him from off her.

"It ain't that easy, sweetie," she said, running her fingers over her clitoris.

"Before we take this any further, we are here to determine will this relationship last a lifetime, or would it end right here... that's totally up to you like I said earlier."

Damn! K-Dog said to himself as he watched Dominique. The way she was working her fingers, inserting them in and out of her pussy, it was driving him insane.

K-Dog knew he had to man up if he wanted to spend the rest of his life with his other half. So, he thought long and hard before speaking.

"Bae, I neva thought in a million years dis day would come. Dom, you know I love you dearly and there's nothing, I won't do for you, boo. But to give up all of dis..." K-Dog spread his hands out towards the sky, emphasizing.

"I had to make my mind up which wasn't an easy thing for me to do. I made enough money than I ever thought I was capable of doin', but I did it. I wanna sit back and enjoy what I sacrificed and worked hard for then to watch it all of it go down the drain. Baby, I wanna thank you for helping me see through dis madness; I couldn't have done dis alone. And for dat very reason, I'll give it all up and spend da rest of my life with you. I'm officially out da game, so help me God." K-Dog got on his knee and pulled out a black box and opened it, pulling out a 10-carat ring. He looked in Dominique eyes and said.

"Will you marry me?" Dominique couldn't believe what she was hearing. She jumped out the bed, still naked and all, and rushed to hug him with tears of joy in her eyes.

"Yes, baby, yes!" K-Dog placed the ring on her fingers while Dominique was caught up planting kisses all over his face. "I can't believe my dreams have finally came true, baby. You don't know what this mean to me, to finally have a family with kids." K-Dog looked like what the hell is she talking about kids.

"Yes, baby, a family... I'm pregnant" she said, rubbing her hands over her stomach.

CHAPTER 12

Killa was feeling like the man of the year as he drove down Sistrunk in his brand-new Bentley. K-Dog had given him the position as head boss, making him the H.N.I.C. over the drug empire. Killa felt like he was a god as he drove up, blasting his music. Just as Killa got to the red light on 27th Avenue, he pulled up, stopping and bobbing his head to the beat. A Benz pulled up on the side of him, slowly letting he window down.

Killa had no idea that Queen was trying to get his attention until she blew the horn. Killa looked over and smiled, showing his iced-out grill.

"Wuz gud, ma?" Killa said as he turned the volume down.

"What you tryna get into?" Queen responded, giving him that look. But just as he was about to reply the light turned green.

"Follow me to 1STOP," Killa said, pulling into the gas station and parking off to the side seconds later.

Once Queen pulled up, she let down the back window of her vehicle, revealing two bad ass bitches in the backseat. They were both butt ass naked, eating each other out. One thing about chicks in Lauderdale, they know how to sniff out a nigga that was making boo-coo money.

Killa knew that Queen was getting mad money because her ol' man left her a few dollars before the feds knocked him off. He already knew that she was on because word traveled fast throughout the streets. Especially for the individuals that were clocking money. However, he didn't know her personally.

All Killa could do was watch as the girls got their freak on. There was no shame in their game. Queen rolled the tinted windows back up. He knew he wasn't fucking with the average bitches that were out here tryna fuck for a couple dollars. Homegirl was about one thing and one thing only…. Big bucks!

"I see you on ya A-game, shawty."

Killa had to respect her gangsta even if he didn't want to.

"Lookie, hea, boo-boo. I stay on that! I'm always on top of my shit believe that playboy."

"Okay then… wuz up? Time is money so wuz gud," Killa said, getting straight to the point. Queen saw how arrogant he was. She made a mental note of that in the back of her head. That's when she decided to go in for the kill.

"Look, boo, take my number down and hit me back later on."

"Bet! I'll do that," Killa said, taking out his phone, so that they can exchange numbers.

"I'ma be looking out for your call," Queen said as she pulled off.

Little did he know Queen had a plan of her own, all she needed was the opportunity to present itself. Then, just like that she was open for game.

Killa had just pulled up to the block on 7th Court in Washington Park just to see how business was going. Killa exited his Bentley, looking like a hood rich rapper. He was draped out in jewelry that cost more than a mansion.

From his teeth to his earlobes, then straight down to his neck and wrist were covered in diamonds.

"Aye! Wea Lil' Coon at, homie?" Killa asked one of his younger workers that were shooting dice with a bunch of other lil' hood niggas on the curb.

"He in the trap. Hold up! I'll go get him," the young hustler said, walking towards the house, in which Killa owned.

While Killa waited for Coon, he observed the motion of the flow as the fiends and hustlers moved on one accord. It kind of reminded him of how it used to be back in the days when he was coming up. The only difference now was the fact that Ms. B was no longer living. So, now her house belonged to Precious and Killa. And that's where all the drugs were being housed.

Moments later, Lil' Coon walked up and gave his mentor a firm handshake.

"What they do, O.G.?"

"I just stopped by to see how thangs was going," Killa said.

"Boss, you know I got er'thing on dis side of town on lock."

"I can dig that, lil' bruh."

While Killa and Lil' Coon were standing up posted against the Bentley, kicking the cool breeze, the raiders pulled up and jumped out on them just to see if anybody would run. But to their surprise nobody moved a muscle. That alone made them 38 hot!

"Keith? I'm sorry, I meant to say "Killa" is that your vehicle, my friend?" one of the raiders said, walking up to him and Coon. Officer Brent was a dirty cop when it came to locking niggas up. If Brent had it out for you best believe he went the whole nine yards to accomplish his goals for locking yo' ass up.

"Is there a problem, Officer Friendly?" Killa said, looking the cracka dead in the eye. Killa had no respect for Officer Brent at all. Shit! If it was up to him, Brent ass would've been dead a long fucking time ago.

"You should be tellin' me. I see you riding around in a brand-new Bentley... fresh off the showroom floor."

"What the fuck that got to do with anything?" Killa said, walking up in his face, showing no fear whatsoever to the most fearful dirty cop. Officer Brent looked around the scenery while smiling. He wanted to arrest Killa and K-Dog so badly his blood boiled, but Officer Brent also knew it wasn't that easy.

"I got ya playboy... oh, and by the way, Mr. Keith, you better watch yo' back, sides, and front because the moment you slip up, I'll be there to rope you with a tight grip." Officer Brent and the other officers jumped into their vehicles and pulled off.

After they left, Killa and Coon did the same and pulled off in Killa's Bentley. Everyone left the scene.

"How much sum'thing like dis cost, Killa?" Lil' Coon asked, admiring the exotic interior of the car.

"Well, in order for a nigga to buy one of these, cash straight off the showroom floor with no payments, lil' bruh, you gotta be a boss ass nigga with sum typa status, lil' bruh," Killa said, passing Coon the blunt.

"Okay, I can dig it, bruh, you already know one day, I'ma buy me one of these just watch what I tell you, big homie. The only difference is, I want mine to be a coupe. Drop top style!"

"You want one of these for real, lil' homie?" Killa asked Coon.

"Hell, yeah, big bruh!" Coon responded a lil' excited.

"I'll tell you what; look in the glove compartment and grab dat." Coon didn't expect to see what he saw when he opened the gloves compartment. He couldn't believe it his eyes. There it was, half a brick, eighteen ounces of pure cocaine.

"What you want me to do with dis, bruh?" Lil' Coon asked.

"Well, you said you wanted to buy one of these, right?"

"Yea, I do."

"Then that's all you, bruh. That's your start right there." Killa looked over at Coon and saw the look oi his face. Knowing that look all too well, he already knew what he was doing in his head…. Numbers!

"So… so how much you want me to bring you back off dis here, big homie?"

"First, do you even know what you holdin' in yo' hands right now, lil' nigga?"

"Naw, not really," Coon said, knowing dam well he did.

"That's a half kilo. Eighteen ounces to be exact."

"What! 18 whole ounces?" He couldn't believe his eyes and ears right now. That's when Killa told him that he didn't owe him shit. Just stay loyal and he'll make sure that he eats good.

All kinds of thoughts started running through Coon's head. He was in deep thought, thinking, adding up all the money he was about to make. Just then, his cell began to ring, interrupting his train of thought.

"Hello, who is dis? Oh, wuz gud, ma? Hell yeah, I'm tryna see you; where you at wit it? Ok, I'm with my homie right now tryna handle sumin'. I'll tell you when to slide thru to the park. Aight! Be easy, baby," Coon said before ending the call just as they pulled in.

Normally around this time of day, the park was packed with hustlers and the kids that loved hanging out there while all the hustlers did their thing. They did that because they knew that the hustlers would buy all they lil' bad ass' ice creams when the ice cream trucks came around.

While Killa and Coon were relaxing in the luxury vehicle, fogging it up with the seats laid back, a blue and black Lexus 350 RX SUV pulled up right next to them. "Hold up, bruh, let me holla at this girl right quick," Coon said, already knowing who was in the SUV that was parked alongside of them. He jumped out and got right into the Lexus.

"Hey, bae, look at you!" the female driver said, showing off her perfect set of teeth.

"What they do, sexy?" he replied while leaning over and kissing her.

"Damn boy! That's how you do it over on this side? You riding around in Bentley's and shit."

"Bae, you know how it goes when you surrounded by niggas that's out here getting money. That's part of the game."

"Yeah, you right about that. But what you got goin on later then bae?" she said, responding while hiking up her skirt to expose her thick thighs. "I wanna show you something so look."

"Girl, I am," Coon said as he watched her continue to lift her skirt further and further until her perfectly shave pussy was showing. She spread her lips, showing him the new piece that was now implanted onto her clitoris.

"Dam, baby! When you got that?" Lil' Coon said, leaning over to get a better look. He damn near had his whole head between her legs at this point. Then he ran his fingers over her clit before inserting them into her love box. Her juices were flowing all over his fingers as he penetrated her tight wet pussy.

"Oooh, bae that feels so good," she said as she opened her legs wider, allowing him full access. "Wat you tryna do make me cum or something?"

He whisked his thumb just a little faster still moving in circular motions while he whispered, "You gonna cum for daddy?"

"Oooh, yes, big daddy... don't stop... keeping going. That's my spot, baby," she said as she started rotating her hips while grinding hard on his fingers. The atmosphere was beginning to get thick and her breath was starting to collapse.

He sure was working his fingers as if he really knew what he was doing. "Baby I'm fena cum... ooooooh, my God!" And within seconds, she was bursting everywhere. Literally, everywhere! Her juices were all over Coon's hands and the fabric from the interior of her car.

"See what you made me do," she said, hitting him on her arm while still climaxing.

"Blame it on me," he said while licking her secretions of his fingers.

"You so nasty, boy!"

"Yeah, I know."

"I taste good don't it, and don't lie either?" she asked while grabbing his hand and licking his fingers too.

"Sum 'thin like dat," he said, teasing her.

He didn't even realize that was kind of an insult, but the way she was feeling good right now, she didn't even care.

"Whatever, boy, when are you gonna stop playing with me Coon? You already know how I feel about you." She started getting in her feelings.

Lil' Coon met Myesha a while back at a restaurant about a year ago. He was feeling her in a major way, but the lifestyle he was living, being that he was a street nigga, had him all caught up. It was kind of hard for him to express how he really felt about her because he lacked emotion. Myesha was an independent woman. She worked at Bank of America, she had her own place and her own car. And to top it all off, she had no kids.

"Listen, Myesha," Coon said. "You know how I feel about you too."

"Okay, then so what are you waiting for? You said you weren't seeing anybody, right?"

"Yeah, he responded."

"So, wuz up?"

All Lil' Coon could do was look out he window. Then he turned around in his seat, facing her. "I never really been in a serious relationship before. All I know is the street life. Being the person who you are, I don't want to hurt you or break your heart. Not saying that's my intentions, but I just want to take it one step at a time." He expressed his feelings the best way he could without hurting her feelings.

"I'ma call you tonight, aight?"

"I guess, boy," she said.

"Aight, then, let me get back to handling my business with big homie." He leaned in and kissed her on the lips before opening the door and getting out of the car.

"Ok, boy; be careful out here," Myesha said, letting the car window down.

"I will," with that said, Lil' Coon walked back to Killa car and got in, only to find him talking on the phone with Queen.

***

Later that day, after Killa dropped Lil' Coon off, he was heading in the City to meet up with Queen. When Killa pulled up in the projects called the Village, there had to be at least fifty niggas hanging out front. It was no pressure for Killa because everybody there knew he wasn't the type of man to be fucked with, but when you're a nigga that's making fetty, you gonna have haters and you gonna have the ones that love you.

As Killa arrived at his destination, a one way in, one way out kind of projects, he parked and got out. Queen's apartment wasn't a far walk at all. As a matter of fact, her door was the first one, which was only steps away. When he walked up, he passed a few niggas that were standing right in front of her building. Out of respect, he spoke as he approached Queen's door and knocked on it. When the door swung open, he saw Queen, standing there bowlegged in a pair of boy shorts. Killa hadn't realized that Queen was that thick. He was astonished as he gazed at the fat camel toe print, he saw sitting high between her legs.

"Hey, Killa, come in," Queen said, smiling at him and admiring the boss nigga she saw standing in her doorway. She stepped to the side to let him in. For some reason, Queen already new that he was the head honcho of a powerful organization. Her plan was to lure him in by enticing him.

"You can have a seat anywhere you'd like," she said while closing and locking her door. Both chicks that he saw freaking each other earlier was there as well, sitting on the sofa, butt ass naked. He didn't waste any time, seating himself between the two chicks.

"I like your set up here," he said. "Its really breathtaking," he said, eyeing the two beautiful women that he placed himself between.

"Why, thank you," she replied. Queen knew it was only a matter of time before she had him eating out of the palm of her hands.

"Now, let's get down to business, shall we?" Queen

took a seat, crossing her legs in an old schooled fashion. "The reason I invited you here is because I know you about getting your money. That makes two of us, and I was wondering can you help me step my game up."

"Listen, baby, I'm the alpha of these streets," he teased her. "It ain't nothing that's too hard for me to do. The real question is, what can I help you with?"

All she could do was smile at the response he just gave her. Now all she needed him to do was be a man of his word and just like that she could execute her plan. "Well, first, I wanna give the king the best time of his life before I present what I have in mind," Queen said, clapping her hands.

"Ladies!"

Stay Alert
K-Dog
CHAPTER 13

Since K-Dog washed his hands with the game, he was spending more and more time with Dominique. They both went on trips and outings together... you know enjoying each other company. It didn't matter what it was Dominique wanted or asked for, K-Dog made it happen, no questions asked.

K-Dog had opened a Boys and Girls Club where the kids could go after school and get help with their homework, and whatever they needed help with. On weekends, K-Dog and the staff members would take the kids on field trips. This was K-Dog's way of giving back to his community, because nowadays the youth needed positive role models. He even talked to them about the street life and how it wasn't the way to go.

As for Dominique, she liked the kids that were at the Boys and Girls Club, they respected her not because she was the founder, that part goes to K-Dog for magically making it happen. The kids loved Dominque because she was more like a mother figure to them, and that's why they loved her.

Some nights tempted K-Dog to hit the streets and what not, but when the thoughts and feeling came to surface, Dominique was right there to help him cope. One night, while K-Dog and Killa were sitting in K-Dog's living room, sipping that good shit, discussing business, pertaining to their legitimate line of work, out the blue Killa went on explaining the details he had with Queen.

K-Dog tried to give Killa good advice about getting out the game while he's still ahead, but Killa were caught up in the fast lane. A lot of times when niggas getting mad money, they become blinded by the money and fame which becomes a lifestyle, turning the dope game into a career. Overlooking the possibilities of going to the Feds and before they know it... Boom! They get hit with the bench.

***

Saturday
10:35 a.m.

K-Dog had just pulled up in his F-250 pickup truck, with his A.T.V.s and dirt bikes. A couple of kids from the Boys and Girls Club came along too. K-Dog did something like this every other weekend. Last week, he took them jet skiing on Hallandale Beach, but this weekend K-Dog decided to take them dirt bike riding.

While the kids were riding around, enjoying themselves for two hours an undercover vehicle pulled up just as K-Dog were loading the bikes back on the truck. Two cops got out and approached K-Dog, who was leaning on his truck.

"My, my, my... who do we have here? If its not the most feared, dangerous, and wealthiest nigger on God's green earth himself," Officer Brent said.

"Wuz up, big tymer?" Officer Brent extended his hand out for K-Dog to shake it.

"Just anotha day," K-Dog responded, accepting the crooked cop hand.

"So, what's bring ya'll round my way?" K-Dog asked, looking them in the eyes.

"You know just to bring you up-to-datc on things, I been watching you and Killa since you fuckers were small fishes, swimming in shark infected water, up to the point y'all made kingpin status. But for some reason, I couldn't run down on y'all, and that's what I hated the most. To be outsmarted by a piece of shit bag niggers." Officer Brent got all up in K-Dog's face, but he remained calm.

"One thing I've learn Officer Brent and Detective Graham, is you neva underestimate your opponent, especially if he's a black man... neva count a black man out." Officer Brent and Detective Graham's faces got so red, that you wouldn't thought both of their heads would've exploded.

"Listen, here you piece of shit, just because you stop pushin' dope, you will never leave the game... you wanna know why?!" officer Brent was talking with his teeth clenched.

"I'll tell you why, because the water is passing your knees. Yeah, muthafucker your ties runs deep. See, I might not be able to get you, but your partner Killa, I'd get him... its just a matter of time. Either way my mission will be completed."

"Well, good luck Officer Friendly on accomplishing yo' mission," K-Dog said, smiling.

"Watch yo' ass, nigga 'cause I'm telling you, if you breathe wrong, I'd be there. And to let you know this is off the record." Both officers turned and walked off, leaving K-Dog to think about what he just said.

Later that night while K-Dog was lying down in his

bed, sleep didn't come easy. The conversation he had with Officer Brent kept replaying in his head repeatedly.

Even though K-Dog was no longer slanging dope, he had to admit that what Officer Brent said about his ties in the game was true. While he was thinking about the conversation, he had with the bitch ass officer, he made a mental note to himself to talk to Killa. All it took was one slip up and everything would come crashing down. Minutes later, sleep finally came over K-Dog's eyes and just like that, he was out like a light.

***

The next morning, while K-Dog was still asleep in the bed, he was moaning very low. Something was feeling so good to him, he thought he was having sex in his dreams. However, this was no dream. Dominique was giving him the best head of his life. She nearly sucked the soul right out of him, but just before that happened, he came in her mouth.

K-Dog opened his eyes only to see his soon-to-be wife with his dick still in her mouth. What a beautiful sight it was to see, he thought to himself as Dominique swallowed his sperm before saying good morning. Then she went further into conversation by saying, "You must've really enjoyed your morning head because you were moaning and shaking at the same time." She started giggling. She climbed on top of him, straddling his naked body. Then she eased herself down real slow on his long hard meat. That tingling sensation that men get while climaxing was still in play when she got on top.

Dominique was full of surprises when it came to sex. She was unpredictable. Her pussy was both warm and wet. Every time K-Dog's dick slid in and out of it as she rode him, you could hear the wetness it had accumulated. Maybe that saying about pregnant women had the best pussy was true. While she rode him, tears fell from her eyes. But these tears weren't sad tears. These tears came because of the immense pleasure she was feeling right now. It was far greater than anything else she'd felt before. Words couldn't describe how good she was feeling in that moment. K-Dog was putting in work with the same energy he put in the streets and it enticed her. As a matter of fact, it was mind blowing! Every time they had sex it was like this.

Now Dominique was at the point of catching her second orgasm. They were coming back to back. Only thing was this time when she came it was nothing like anything she experienced before. Her whole body turned cold then got stiff. While her eyes rolled in the back of her head, her body locked up on her. This orgasm scared K-Dog because he thought he either did some damage or he harmed her in some way.

"Baby, are you okay?" he asked nervously as he got up. Dominique was not responding. Honestly, K-Dog didn't know what to do, but seconds later, she came back to her normal self.

"I'm ok, honey," she said, finally while curling up into the fetal position.

"What happened to you? I thought you were dying on me," K-Dog said. But, to his surprise Dominique started smiling.

Then she said, "I don't know babe this never happened before." She continued by telling him that if he ever gave that good dick to anyone besides her and she found out, she'd …

But that's when he K-Dog cut her off and finished her sentence by saying, "I'D KILL YOU!"

Slippers Count
Friday the 13th
Killa
CHAPTER 14

Around this time of year, a lot of shit got ugly. Especially in the hood. People usually came up missing. Many were dying; and the crime rate when up at least 90 percent, fast too.

Killa was home playing with his daughter Rayanna, when Queen hit his phone. They'd been doing business for about four months now. Killa never suspected Queen to be a C.I. but little did he know, she was! She was working for the feds at that. Big time shit, not no little sheriff's department snitch. The Feds were supplying Queen with the cash to buy the dope from Killa and she was copping at least four to five bricks from him every two weeks. They were building a case and she was providing everything they needed for them to take him down.

Today, was the day for her to re-up from him, but he had no idea she was setting him up. At 3:45 p.m., Killa pulled into the parking lot of the super Wal-Mart on Oakland and 441. Queen never met Killa in locations like this before. However, the thought that she was setting him up never crossed his mind. The money was too right for Killa to even think she was a confidential informant. For that very reason it blinded him. Y'all know the saying. "Every dog has its day." And today just happened to be Killa's.

Once Killa pulled in the parking space and parked. It was only a few minutes later before Queen pulled up and parked beside him. She exited her vehicle and walked over to his. He got out as well.

"Wuz up, sweetie," she said as he greeted him with a hug.

"You know me, baby, always grindin'," Killa responded.

The active vicinity was packed with loyal customers. People were coming and going just as they would any other day. That was the perfect screen of smoke for distraction. Killa popped open his trunk and grabbed the duffle bag that contained the narcotics in it. Five bricks of pure raw cocaine. Queen walked back towards her vehicle and grabbed hold of a big brown paper bag from off her backseat. She gave it to Killa for an even exchange of the goods.

"This deal is sealed," she said, speaking into her hidden microphone, giving her colleagues the code after the transaction was completed.

"What?" Killa said, looking confused.

"Killa, I'm so sorry, but I had to do what I had to do," she said while stepping back out of his reach just in case. Only moments later, it dawned on him that this bitch was setting him up.

"Bitch, you really set me up, after all I did for yo' ass?" Killa reached under his shirt, grabbing his .40 from his waistband. He pointed it dead at Queens' head.

"I'm sorry, Killa, but you wouldn't have understood my situation," Queen pleaded for her life, hoping that Killa wouldn't end it right there. While this was going on, all the bystanders were trying to get out of the crossfire. They were screaming, running, and ducking behind vehicles. Queen had tears rolling from her eyes.

Where are they, she thought to herself. Everything started slowing down.

"I wouldn't understand you setting me up, taking me away from my family, bitch. That's what I wouldn't understand. Naw it ain't goin' down like dis hoe." Killa cocked his gun back, allowing one bullet to be in the head. Then he snatched Queen by her throat. Right before Killa was about to pull the trigger, the feds came out of nowhere. They surrounded them with all kinds of powerful rifles

"Freeze! Drop your weapon and put your hands in the air," the federal agent yelled.

"Please, don't kill me, Killa," Queen begged. She knew he didn't give a fuck about these crackas and their weapons. "All I was trying to do was free my ol' man that's it."

"Bitch, shut the fuck up," Killa advised her as he looked around at all the agents who had him surrounded.

"DROP YOUR WEAPON AND PUT YOUR HANDS IN THE AIR!" another one yelled. Queen was still pleading for her life because she knew he would take it either way. Even the feds were trying to talk some sense into him. The standoff lasted about fifteen minutes before Killa realized that he was in a loss-loss situation. Killa released Queen and lowered his weapon, dropping it on the ground before putting his hands in the air.

The FBI agents rushed Killa, kicking the gun away from him while placing him in handcuffs. They then escorted him to the patrol vehicle they had sitting alongside the back of both his and Queen's car. Once they got everything under control, they pulled off, leaving Killa's vehicle behind for towing.

So much shit was going through Killa's head while he was being transported to the station. Killa was hurting because he remembered the promise that he made to Precious about never allowing anything to take him away from her and Rayanna. He couldn't believe the way he allowed pussy and money to cloud his vision and take away his freedom. The situation at hand was eating him alive as he kept replaying the conversation, he had with K-Dog. All that didn't matter now because Killa fucked up. And he knew he fucked up badly. The only thing he could do now was hold his head down and pray for the best.

Thirty minutes later, Killa pulled up to the station with the feds about forty deep. Channel 7 News was also on the scene, filming live. News reports were trying their best to get clear shots of the kingpin as he was escorted inside. Once inside, they stripped searched Killa before throwing him into a cold ass room for hours. This was their way of breaking you down mentally before beginning the questioning.

"Have you ever seen First 48?" This was the tactic strategy they used before milking you like a cow for information. Killa sat in a room, that had to be at least fifty degrees for at least four hours before they finally took him out and placed him into another freezing room. This one was the one used for the interrogation. They were hoping that he'd break just like the other "so-called" gangsters they've had before. But not only did Killa hold his own, he also stuck to the g-code.

They did everything in their power to make him break, but nothing worked. They even went as far as turning off the camera's and beating him. Still, Killa kept it all the way G. He sold the Feds a total of eighteen kilos of cocaine. They had pictures and audio video of him and

Queen, making numerous transactions on various occasions.

He couldn't believe what he was seeing in front of him. They had him caught red-handed like a kid, sneaking and getting caught with his hands in a cookie jar. After seeing all the evidence, they had on him Killa look the agent's dead in the eye and said, "Show me my cell."

***

Broward County Main Jail...

Killa was sitting in the bookie cell, waiting to be processed into the system once again, but this time Killa knew he was facing a lot of time. They had Killa all over the news like he was Al Capone or something.

"The kingpin, Keith Thomas known as Killa was arrested by the F.B.I. today on multiple charges. And if convicted he could he could get life," the new reporter said as Killa watched the television that was in his cell.

"Shit!" Killa said as he got up and went to the phone to make a one free call. The first person Killa decided to call was... Precious.

"Hello."

"Precious, wuz up, baby?"

"Boy! Yo' face is all over da muthafuckin' news."

"Yeah, I know, but don't worry. I got dis under control."

"Under control?! Boy, how da fuck you got sum'thing under control when they got yo' goddamn face and name under da title... Kingpin!" Precious was giving it to Killa's ass.

"Do you have a bond?" Precious asked.

"Naw, not yet, but I need for you to contact K-Dog and my lawyer. And let them know my situation."

"K-Dog already know and he's taking care of dat now... Killa, I can't believe dis shit is happenin'." Precious started crying.

"Baby, listen, everythin is gonna be okay. I'ma need for you to be strong for me and Rayanna, you think you could do dat for me?"

"I guess," was all Precious could say.

"Aight, then, bae. I gotta go, okay?"

"Aight, Killa. I love you."

"I love you too," with that said, Killa ended the call and went back to his seat under the television where his face was glued.

Words of Advice
Two Weeks Later
K-Dog
CHAPTER 15

If only Killa would've listen to K-Dog when he tried to tell Killa about getting out the game, he wouldn't be in the predicament he's in now. K-Dog was trying to pull all the right strings to make Killa's situation better.

The judge had denied Killa bond, saying that not only was Killa a flight risk, but he was a threat to society. Even though K-Dog was still being harassed by Officer Brent and Detective Graham, he was still gonna be there for his righthand man Killa.

A couple of days ago while K-Dog was locking up his car lot, the same dick heads Officer Brent and Detective Graham came to his place of business, informing him that all the murders and blood shedding he left behind wasn't cleaned up properly that it was just a matter of time before it caught up with him. And that's what K-Dog feared the most.

Killa was sitting in the living room, watching B.E.T. when his phone rang. K-Dog already knew it was Killa calling from the County by the ring tone. K-Dog picked up.

"Wuz gud, gangsta?"

"I'm gud, homie, just waiting for my court date."

"You think them crackers gonna do sum 'thing for you, my boy?" K-Dog asked, already knowing the question to the answer.

"I don't know, bruh, for real."

"Wat yo' lawyer talkin' 'bout? Is he talkin' gud on yo' behalf or wat?"

"You know he tryna do his best and what not. But, with my little situation the feds got me and they ain't lettin' up one bit."

K-Dog listened to Killa's every word as Killa explained how the Feds had him by his balls. Deep down, K-Dog knew the system was corrupt. And if the price was right, maybe... just maybe Killa would could walk.

They two talked until the phone call ended. Just as K-Dog ended the call, Dominique came walking into the living room with her hand on her hips. Her stomach was getting bigger each day.

"Is everything ok, sweetie?" Dominique asked, walking up behind K-Dog, massaging his neck. She sensed something was going on with her man.

"Yes, babe, I'm good... I just got off the phone with Killa," K-Dog responded while relaxing as Dominique was working her fingers. "Damn! Girl, this shit feels good." K-Dog closed his eyes as Dominique did her thang.

"I know," she said, smiling.

"Oh, yeah? So, what else you good with?"

Dominique was thinking to herself before saying, "Well, let's see.... Mmmmn! I'm good at knowing how to keep my man satisfied." She stopped massaging K-Dog's neck and walked in front of him kneeling between his legs, unzipping his pants. Dominique reached into his pants, pulling out his already erected dick and placing it into her mouth. Dominique was a lady in the streets, but a freak in the streets. She always carried herself in a well-respected manner. However, when it came down to pleasing her man in the sheets, baby was a stone-cold freak, and he loved it. Dominique sucked K-Dog off reeeaaallll good until he released into her mouth; swallowing every drip he was produced. Once she was done, she got up and walked away, leaving K-Dog in his thoughts. Damn! K-Dog thought to himself as he watched Dominique walk off.

***

Nobody was able to locate Queen or find out her whereabouts. It's like she fell off the face of God's green earth. Queen's disappearance startled K-Dog in the worse way. He needed to find her so that he could have her taken out. If he got Queen killed, it would weaken the case against Killa by reducing the circumstantial evidence that the Feds had on him. By killing Queen that would have made Killa's conviction slim to none. Eliminating the victim would only mean no witness, no case.

K-Dog pulled up on the Ave. at Friendly Store in Franklin Park where Lil' Coon and his clique were hanging out. Big Dre, Lil' Dre, Rich Kid, C-Murder, Sleepy, and the rest of the original boys known as D.P.G. (Dog Pound Gangstas). They were all posted up. It's been a while since K-Dog hit the block up on this side of town. Franklin was the bottom of the trenches where niggas played for only one thing... keeps! Instead of letting K-Dog get out of his vehicle, Lil' Coon stopped shooting dice and walked up to him once seeing the Rover pull in.

"Wuz up, big homie?" Lil' Coon said while giving K-Dog dap.

"Wuz gud, lil' homie?"

"Dat's wuz up. So, wat brings you to these dangerous grounds?" Lil' Coon asked.

K-Dog couldn't believe that this lil' nigga had the audacity to ask him some shit like. Let me get this jit straight right quick, K-Dog thought to himself. "Lil' Coon check dis out, right?" K-Dog opened the door and got out. "Don't get it twisted. I'm still that nigga! And dis street shit runs deep in my blood homie. Don't think for a second, I laid down because I backed up outta the game. I made a lot of money. I saw a lot of thangs about this lifestyle. It only ends two ways, death or prison. This fame we out here chasin; da cars, da money, da clothes, and the pretty bitches don't mean shit. Er'thang you made or sacrificed to get those thangs will be taken away in the blink of an eye."

K-Dog was trying to give him something to think about because he actually cared about Lil' Coon. It's more to life than trapping and popping pistols. However, this is one of the few things that goes on in the hood. Also, this is what the youths see while growing up. Parents who pay little attention to their children lose them to the streets. It's a parents' job to lead and show them by setting the example of how they should live.

"I hear ya, big homie, but dis all I know. I don't know how it feels to have a positive role model, so I do what I do regardless the cost. If it's meant for me to die out here on the streets, then it is what it is." Lil' Coon was talking from the heart. "To be honest, the only person I look u to as a role model is you, Killa."

"I hear ya, lil' homie, and I respect what you said. Now the reason I called you is because I was wondering did you see or hear anything about Queen?"

"Naw man, I haven't seen her since the Feds ran down on Killa."

"Alright then, keep ya eyes and ya ears open," K-Dog said. "If you hear anything let me know." K-Dog opened the door to his vehicle and got in.

"I gotcha, big homie," Lil' Coon said as he gave K-Dog dap.

"So, how's business goin' out hea wit' you?" K-Dog said, changing the subject.

"Oh, shit gud, bruh. I got er'thang under control out hea. And shit still runnin' like Killa had it." K-Dog already knew Coon was telling the truth because the bookkeeper kept K-Dog on point.

"Alright, then lil' nigga, let me get goin'."

"Be easy, big homie. Let me get back to this money."

Lil' Coon walked off as K-Dog pulled off, heading towards Sunrise on McDonald's street. Moments later, K-Dog was driving west on Sunrise, an undercover car hit the blue and red lights, pulling him over. K-Dog pulled inside of the BP gas station on Sunrise Blvd and 31st Ave. which was only yards away from the Swap Shop. When K-Dog pulled into the BP gas station, he parked and waited for the officer to approach. K-Dog was looking through the rearview mirror only to find Officer Brent and his partner Detective Graham, getting out of the vehicle.

"SHIT!" K-Dog said as they walked up, knocking on both windows.

"You must think yo' shit don't stank muthafucka. I told you if you breathe wrong, I'ma be there. What you thought, it was a game?" Officer Brent said.

"One down and one more to go muthafucka," Detective Graham said before walking back to the car with his partner. "We gonna get yo' ass one way or another."

"Fuck man!" K-Dog said, hitting the steering wheel as the officers passed by with the windows down, flicking K-Dog the bird.

Stressing
Monday 11:45 a.m.
Killa
CHAPTER 16

C ourt was in session at the Broward County main courthouse, and Killa was sitting and waiting for the judge to call his name. precious, K-Dog, along with family and friends were also present. They all were hoping the judge granted Killa's motion, and give him a bond.

Rayanna was crying for her daddy, wanting him to pick her up and hold her, it gotten so bad Precious had to take her out the court room.

Killa's attorney was late as he walked into the court-room, stopping briefly to talk to Precious, explaining Killa's situation to her the best way he knew. Shortly after, Killa's attorney got finish talking with Precious, he made his way to where Killa and the few Detainees were, in the box. As soon as he approached the box, the judge called his name.

"Your Honor, give us a few, I just literally walked through the door. Can you give me a second to talk to my client?"

"Go ahead," the judge said with attitude, looking at Killa with that evil look in his eyes.

Moments later, his attorney finished talking with him, he approached the bench.

"Your Honor Keith Thomas on page six, CF-2001302..." he waited for the judge to catch up before continuing. "All the way down at the bottom. The reason we are here today because umm... I put a motion in for a bond, on the behalf of my client. Who were charged with selling to a federal C.I. Your Honor as you can see, Mr. Thomas family is here to support him along with his child who was born a few months ago. Your Honor, my client is willing to pay whatever for a bond, just set a price and its done. And if you grant this motion, Your Honor, I ask you to put him on house arrest until further noticed. Please, Your Honor, I'm asking for a favor on this one." Killa's attorney looked the judge dead in the eyes like his life depends on it.

"Is there's anything else you like to say?" the judge asked Killa's attorney.

"That's it for right now, Your Honor."

"State, what would you like to say, do you agree or disagree upon, Mr. Thomas getting bond?" the state of attorney stood to his feet.

"Well, Your Honor, that would not be appropriated, Mr. Thomas did sell the F.B.I. twenty kilos of pure cocaine. And I mean pure!" the state attorney said, rubbing his nose.

"Fifteen!" Killa's attorney yelled out, interrupting the federal state attorney.

"Regardless if it was ten, its still a very high-profile case, not to mention, Mr. Thomas was also in possession of a firearm, which was used while committing a crime, making it a level (9), punishable by life. Also, Your Honor, Mr. Thomas has a criminal record, so I totally disagree with the motion." The State sat back down while sipping his coffee.

"Okay, since I heard from both sides, I just wanted thank you for being here today. But as you all know the law is the law and that's what I stand firm on." The judge looked around, observing the entire courtroom before speaking again.

"Your motion for bond, Mr. Brown, has been denial."

"Wat da fuck! Oh, hell naw!" The whole courtroom had gotten out of control, they couldn't believed the judge had denial Killa's bond after everything was paid off.

"Order in the court! Order in the court!" The judge banged the gavel, trying everything in his power to get the courtroom under control. But the peoples weren't having that. All types of out bursts were yelled, the guards had to escort Killa out the courtroom and take him back to the holding cell, with the rest of them clowns.

"Thomas, you need to hold that noise down," one of the officers said.

"Fuck you! Suck my dick you bitch ass Uncle Tom mafucka!" Killa said, disregarding the deputy orders.

"Roll G-4," the officer said after putting on a pair of gloves. All the other inmates stepped to the side as the deputy walked into the holding cell.

"Mr. Thomas, you need to calm the fuck down, and I ain't going to tell you no more," the deputy said as he approached Killa.

"Wat you gonna do, fuck boy? Beat me?" Killa took off his uniform shirt and got into the deputy face.

"I ain't got nothing to lose, nigga. What you wanna do?" Just as the deputy was getting ready to lay hands in Killa, a female deputy who was a sergeant recognized Killa stepped up.

"Deputy Moore, I got it from here." Sergeant knew she had to move fast and get everything under control, because if she didn't, they were going to beat the shit out of him.

Deputy Moore looked at Killa, then at the female Sergeant, then back at Killa.

"You sho, Sergeant?" he asked.

"Yes, Deputy Moore, now can you leave please!" She waited for Deputy to walk out before turning around, facing Killa who had no clue who the hell she was. Killa looked at her and said to himself, This couldn't be.

"Look, Mr. Thomas, I know your situation, but acting out ain't going to get you nowhere. So, just chill out, and I'll take you back to your floor, okay?" All Killa did was looked at her as he calmed down. Once the Sergeant saw that Killa was good, she walked out the cell, closing the door back. Killa couldn't believe what he just seen. Ms. Roberts, who Killa had given a ride to, granddaughter was a sergeant at the Broward County Jail. Damn, how crazy was this.

Thirty minutes later, the holding cell door rolled back, and Bray walked in, calling Killa's name.

"Keith Thomas!"

"Yeah!" Killa stood up and approached her.

"Step out the cell and put your hands behind your back." Killa did what he was told, while Bray put the handcuffs on his wrist for safely purpose, and escorted Killa back to his floor.

Bray felt sorry for Killa because she knew what blacks went through, especially the black men. She watched time and time again as they got railroaded. All Bray could do was hope for the best in Killa's situation.

Nightmares
K-Dog
CHAPTER 17

ominique was finally bringing their 1st child into the world, and K-Dog had to stand by Dominique side and watched her birth their son. Seeing her virginal open the way it did, was the hardest thing K-Dog had to do.

After the delivery was over, K-Dog was able to hold his firstborn son, happiness was written all over K-Dog's face. The look in his eyes, Dominique knew he would be a great father.

Two days after Dominique gave birth to their child; she was discharge and allowed to go home with her son little Javon who weighed 8 ½ pounds.

K-Dog stayed by Dominique's side for three whole days, making sure she had everything. Whenever Lil' Javon cried K-Dog rushed to his side every time, spoiling him rotten. All K-Dog had to do was pick Lil' Javon up and just like that he'd stop crying.

One night while K-Dog were sleeping, he was having a bad dream which turned into a nightmare. K-Dog was dreaming he were at the car lot, sitting in his office, when a young kid stepped into his office. The kid had to be around twenty to twenty-one, even his face resembles somebody, but K-Dog couldn't put a finger on it. All he remembered in the heat of the moment was the kid pulling out a gun and shooting him multiple times.

"Bae, wake up... stop fighting me and get up!" Dominique was trying to wake K-Dog up.

"Ooh, my God, baby... get up." Dominique shook him until he finally woke up.

"Baby, are you okay?"

K-Dog sighed before speaking. "Yeah, bae, I'm gud. I just had a dream that a kid walked into my officer and shot me, bae." K-Dog was drench in sweat.

"Baby, come here." Dominique reached out, hugging him.

"All it was a dream, nothing more, baby. Now lay back down and get some rest."

"Bae, dat shit felt real, I'm tellin' you." K-Dog laid back down, and within minutes, he was drifting back to sleep.

***

It was a Tuesday night and it was storming like crazy, and the streets were flooded with water. You couldn't drive from point A to point B without driving 5 m.p.h., but still, that didn't stop K-Dog from calling a meeting.

Over fifty members were gathered at a secluded location. However, the address was only given to the members of The Takeover. Those members were the only ones allowed to come. K-Dog stood in the middle of the crew, dressed in all-black as he gave his speech.

"The reason we're all here tonight and not laying up in some pussy or home with our families is because we have a serious problem," he stated. He then looked around observing all his members. Then he continued. "All we know is that Killa's been taken into custody by the Feds and it's our own job to find out where Queen is and kill her ass right where she standin' at. I want this bitch dead ASAP! And I won't stop until she is." K-Dog pulled a folder filled with pictures of the same officers that tried to put him in confinement with Killa.

"These are the muthafuckas that I want dead by next week." K-Dog went over everything with his crew. Detail for detail, explaining exactly how he wanted the job done. One thing about K-Dog was he was a master at finding out information. It wasn't hard for him to get the info he wanted either.

***

K-Dog and Dominique were sitting in the living room, watching Love & Hip-Hop when the breaking news report interrupted their quality time. Krystal Lockhart was a bad ass red-boned news reporter. Standing at about 5'9" with long thick wavy hair. Everything about her attire said one thing and one thing only... she was high maintenance. She stood there beautiful as ever, ready to give her latest report.

"Hi everyone, we are live tonight because of a deadly homicide. Two officers of the law were killed today. The first one was named Michael Brent. He served on the force for nearly thirteen years and he was gunned down today by some unknown gangsters. Reports show that the weapon used to kill him was an AK 47 assault rifle. The second victim was none other than the well-known Detective John Smith. He served on our city's force for nine-and-a-half years. He was also shot multiple times by the same weapon that took out officer Brent. The officers were ambushed from both sides in their patrol vehicles. No evidence was left behind except the bullet shells which had no fingerprints attached.

"Anyone who might know who these attackers are or have any information on finding the people who caused this deadly tragedy, please call 1-800-TIP-LINE. There is a $50,000 reward for anyone who has information on these heartless, brutal gangsters. We are coming to you live from the incident scene. This is reporter Krystal Lockhart with Channel 7 News, signing off."

After the newsflash ended, K-Dog began smiling from ear to ear like the grinch who stole Christmas. Getting rid of the cops was a good thing because now his life could go back to normal. Going back to jail was a factor that no longer belonged in his equation.

Later that day, K-Dog felt like a brand-new man. It was like he had risen from the dead and walked straight out of his grave. As he pulled up to one of the corner stores on the Ave, he felt relieved. As a matter of fact, he felt so good, he started dishing out money to all the little kids that happened to be there at that moment.

Lil' Coon slid up on him, knowing that he was in a great mood. "Somebody's feelin' like the man of the year, ain't he? Did Santa stop by earlier today?" Lil' Coon said, laughing while giving K-Dog dap.

"Man, God is good," K-Dog said, putting his hands in the air and waving like he was rejoicing in church.

"Bruh, that shit was like taking candy from a baby. Them cock suckas was eating donuts and drinkin' coffee when me and my niggas slid up on 'em. They ain't even have time to make a wish before I sent them to meet the creator," Coon said feeling cocky.

"Yeah, y'all boys did that! Straight swiss cheesed they

ass," K-Dog said, giving Coon a brotherly hug.

"Dawg, it's all good, bruh. You already know how I get down... murder, murder, murder... shoot first, then ask question later," Lil' Coon responded.

Bloody Tragedy
Killa
CHAPTER 18

Killa had been locked up for about a year and a half now. The courtroom was filled with his beloved family and friends. Today was the first day of his trial because he refused to take the offer, which was a mandatory forty years to door. In Killa's mind, if they wanted him to do forty years, they would have to give it to him. He wasn't volunteering himself for no time.

Killa entered the courtroom in a white Versace suit with matching all-white Versace shoes. As Bray escorted him to his seat, she had to admit that he looked damn good. She had already promised him that if it came to trial, then she would be the only one to escort him in. She kept that promise.

Once Killa was seated, his attorney approached him. The two of them went over a few details pertaining to how the opening and closing were planned to go. Precious and Rayanna, along with the rest of the crew, sat directly behind him. Nobody has seen or heard from Queen still. That made Killa feel uneasy in his seat. The key witness was still out there somewhere. And deep down, Killa knew his chances of walking away a free man with her still alive was zero to none. But, regardless of what happened, he made peace with his mind and he was ready to pay the price.

As the federal judge approached the bench by coming through his side chamber, the bailiff said, "All rise, court is now in session. Now is the time to turn off all phones and computer devices. The honorable Judge Victor Tobin is now present."

"Good morning Judge," he turned and said, facing Victor.

"Good morning," the judge said as he took his seat and faced all the people who were present on behalf of Killa.

Trial lasted four days before the jury was able to come forth with a verdict. During all four days of trial, the representatives of the Attorney General's office brought forth everything possible they could find on Killa. But what broke the back of the camel is when Queen walked in and took the stand.

Then it all began to make sense. The reason no one could find her was because the Feds had her in witness protection. They must've had her underground somewhere. Killa's attorney put up a damn good fight from beginning to end. However, when they have you by the balls it's difficult to get the jury to side on the defendant's behalf.

After the state and Killa's attorney closed their final arguments, the jury was able to go into their delegation room. They lasted forty-five minutes before coming back into the courtroom.

Killa had already set his mind that they found him guilty. There was no way in hell he would be walking away a free man when the state had all this evidence against him.

The bailiff took the piece of paper from the jury and handed it to the judge. Of course, the verdict read guilty. When the judge received the piece of paper, he looked at it, and smiled before putting it down.

The jury have reached the verdict. Mr. Thomas on count 1, distribution of narcotics, count 2, conspiracy to operation of organized crime, and count 3 possession of a firearm. The people in the courtroom were still waiting to hear his response, but then he continued to read until he got to count 8.

"Well, Mr. Thomas, the jury has found you guilty on all charges and counts," said the judge. Just like that, Killa's freedom was taken away from him. Really and truly his family was hurt the most. What else could Killa do other than put his head down and close his eyes, knowing he wasn't going to see the streets or his family again? The entire audience was in a state of shock because even Bray's grandmother, Ms. Roberts took the stand on Kila's behalf. She told the jury how she first met him and how he's really a good person.

Precious broke down and cried out as if he was killed or something. As for K-Dog, he got up and left the courtroom when he heard the verdict. For him, it was now time to put plan B into effect. There were all sorts of reporters outside, waiting to question anyone that was willing to talk to them. Ms. Roberts was giving a statement to one of the reporters, when being interrupted by the FBI that was escorting Queen. That's when the reporters rushed towards her and one asked her, "Ms. Clark, now that the drug kingpin was sentence to life without parole, thanks to you, what would you like to say?" Queen couldn't say anything as she looked into the lens of the camera, facing her.

Just then, a shot was fired by a sniper rifle. The bullet

hit Queen dead in the center of her frontal lobe, knocking her brains all over the camera's. Bullseye! Everyone ran for cover because no one wanted to be the innocent bystander. They ran for nothing because not another shot was ever fired, except the one that killed Queen. No one knew where the shot came from. The FBI and the local police were looking high and low to see exactly which direction the shooter was in. But, they came up with nothing except instead a dead informant.

It took the police department hours to get everything under control. Channel 7 News was live on set again, talking to Pastor Roberts. "Hi, this is Shakita Cooks coming to you live from the front end of the Broward County courthouse. Just hours ago, a key witness to the epic drug lord, kingpin investigation, was shot in cold blood by a high-powered assault rifle. The weapon used was the same type of weapon like the one's used in previous unsolved murders. We've come to believe that the killing had everything to do with Keith Thomas, a.k.a, the kingpin in this case. Here, I have standing with me, Pastor Roberts, the person who was standing directly in front of Vickie Clark before she was murdered."

Ms. Roberts didn't mind being in the spotlight at all. As a matter of fact, she loved being the center of attention, even when she preached at church. "So, Pastor Roberts, can you please tell us what you saw from your perspective?"

"Lord have mercy!" Ms. Roberts said, looking into the camera while holding her head to the sky and shaking it. "It was a horrible ugly scene. I was standing not too far from that poor child, when that shot was fired. It came out the blue. I saw that poor child's head explode right in front my very eyes. Whomever did this to her was just pure evil," she said. As Ms. Pastor Roberts finished her statement, she said, "But one thing I do know is you reap what you sow, and God don't like ugly."

Later that night, while Killa was laying in his bunk, talking on the smartphone Bray had managed to get him, his cell door clicked. He thought it was a "shakedown" moment. That was the first thing that came to his mind, so he hurried up and stashed his pipeline before steeping out. To his surprise Bray was in the control booth, standing there with a smile from ear to ear, telling him to come on out. Killa stepped forward out of the cell and into the hallway, looking for the other deputies. But there was none. Bray came out of the control booth and starting walking towards a utility closet that kept all the cleaning supplies.

Killa wasn't sure what Bray had in mind until she opened the supply room and turned off the lights. Soon, as he stepped in behind her, she started kissing him all over ferociously. It was almost like she was hungry and he the meal. She wasted no time taking full control of his body. In her mind, the situation was acceptable because she waited a long time for that moment. Ever since she laid eyes on Killa she wanted him in a worse way.

As Bray was kissing Killa, she began to massage his manhood at the same time. Soon after, she pulled his dick out really to do her magic, but she paused for a moment because she couldn't believe what she was seeing. This man was packing, she thought to herself.

"Damn!" she said. Then, she immediately fell to her knees and placed all of his double Garcia-sized man sausage into her mouth. She took him in inch by inch until his entire shaft was deep in her throat. Killa grabbed the back of her head like every man does when they get caught up in the moment of some great head. More than anything, she wanted to feel him inside of her. Urgently, she stopped giving him head right before he was about to bust and began unbuckling her belt and pulling her pants down. Without any hesitation Killa went into action. He turned her around and bent her over while licking her from the back.

Once she was soaking wet, Killa entered her damp, slushy, moist, vagina. He began to fuck her hard like this was the last pussy left on earth and it belonged to him. It's been awhile since he got his rocks off upon being incarcerated. Other than masturbation, he didn't really worry about getting pussy anyway because he was always in the streets. Shit! Look where pussy got him now.

Bray was relaxed, knowing that she had everything under control. Killa, on the other hand, was more worried about getting caught. In less than five minutes, they both climaxed. Afterwards, they both got right, then exited the storage room, going their separate ways. When Killa got back to his cell, he laid down with a big smile on his face. He didn't know that getting real pussy while being locked up was possible. He felt like a champ as he closed his eyes and went to sleep.

K-Dog
CHAPTER 19

Ootne thing about a nigga that's used to getting mad money on the streets, it's hard to turn away from the game 100% regardless of what the situation is. It doesn't necessarily have to be about drugs.

K-Dog was involved in the "bulldog game." Which is just another term for dog fighting. This was his way of making legit money. He and Lil' Coon became inseparable since his indictment. Lil' Coon was moving up fast in the drug game since he became the one in charge of the Takeover Empire. K-Dog molded him from the inside out. And he taught him how everything should be running. Coon was only twenty years old, but he was also very bold when it came to his line of work. Lil' Coon was also involved in bull dogging.

Today was a big match for his best dog. The payout for this match was $60,000. Hitman was his top dog and anytime he brought him out it was guaranteed the top dollar. Hitman was the grand champion when it came to ranking a pure-bred fighter who never lost a match.

Down south in Miami, deep in Homestead was where the match was being held. Lil' Coon and K-Dog were already standing amongst the crowds, waiting for their opponent to arrive. Coon kept Hitman between his legs while inside the pit, getting ready for the face off. Literally! Shortly after, it was showtime. That's when Coon turned Hitman around, so that he can face off with his opponent. On the referee's count of three, the dogs were released.

Hitman charged headfirst, fast and low just like his master. Weighing approximately thirty-eight pounds he was all muscle and in topnotch shape for a dog his age and size. Off the scratch, Hitman flipped the other dog by using his head, causing the canine to fall backwards and land flat on his back. He wasted no time, grabbing his rival under the windpipe like a lion would do when going in for the kill.

Coon already knew the fight wouldn't have lasted longer than forty minutes. Hitman had gotten a firm grip when biting down and cutting off his rival's airway which stopped him from breathing.

"Y'all country ass niggas can get that bread up, it's game time, baby," Lil' Coon said.

"It ain't over yet, nigga!" Dude responded before looking back at his dog. Hitman applied straight pressure on the dog's throat. The crowd was going bananas as the witnessed the beat down. Hitman was hungry. He acted as if he hadn't eaten in months the way he was brutally beating the other dog.

"Come on, Tiger, get that shit right for daddy. Don't let me down!" Dude yelled out, hoping his voice would trigger something that would make Tiger get himself out of the trouble he was currently facing. Tiger was trying with everything in his power to break free from Hitman's monster grip. However, nothing was working. Hitman had monster jaws and every time Tiger tried, he applied even more pressure. Both Lil' Coon and K-Dog began cheering

Hitman on even more because they knew he was on the verge on annihilating his opponent.

"Oh, shit!" Lil' Coon said as he watched Hitman shake Tiger by his throat as if he were a rag doll. "Y'all better break it up if y'all want this muthafucka to live because I'm telling ya now, he not gonna make it," Lil' Coon said to Tiger's owner.

"Man fuck that shit! Let Hitman kill it. I got plenty more," Dude said, trying to act like watching his baby die wasn't phasing him one bit. He knew dam well Tiger was his best dog. Lil' Coon sparked up a blunt as he watched Hitman draw Tiger's last breath. That was another body count under Hitman's belt, making it number twenty-eight.

In less than twenty minutes, the fight was over, and Tiger was as dead as a doorknob. Hitman still wasn't trying to stop even though he knew that his rival was already dead. K-Dog went around, collecting all the wins while Coon went over to get break Hitman apart from Tiger.

***

The rapper, B.G., was having a concert at the Voodoo Lounge in downtown Las Olas. K-Dog and Lil' Coon decided to hit up the Flea Market off Oakland and 31st Ave. They were trying to cop some fits to wear to the concert later that night. While they were there, they wanted to holla at some pretty bitches.

The Flea was packed from with people from the parking lot to the inside of the small building. When they walked inside, all eyes were on them like they were stars. They didn't even make it in the building good before they bumped into Precious, walking hand and hand with some other nigga.

K-Dog was surprised when he saw her, holding hands

with this nigga like they been together forever. When Coon saw this shit, he instantly wanted to lay hands on buddy, but K-Dog stopped him.

"Let that bitch be," K-Dog said.

"If Killa was out I could bet he'd break her and that nigga neck," Coon responded while giving Precious the evil eye.

"Listen, lil' homie bitches ain't shit. Especially if you a nigga out here in the streets getting money. They gon' fuck with you, but the moment you get locked up or go to prison, they'll leave yo' ass so fast it'll make yo' head explode. Always remember that as long as you live nothing good nothing lasts forever. My daddy told me that shit right there, nigga. Come on, dawg, let's do us up in this bitch, fuck that dog ass hoe."

***

The Voodoo Lounge was on swole. Everyone there was getting their ball on, until the Takeover clique entered the building. They shut everything down. Coon and K-Dog were both dressed in the finest designer Robin jeans outfits. To top it off, they were rocking some iced out ass jewels. They came in about fifty deep, and they posted up in their own section. Fine wine and champagne bottles were scattered throughout their tables. You could smell the fancy colognes and hi-grade coming from their area.

B.G. was onstage doing his thing with his Choppa City niggas. He even gave K-Dog a special shout out, saying, 'real niggas recognize real niggas.' Bitches were trying their best to push up on anybody that was apart of the Takeover clique because hey knew them boys had duffle bags full of dough. On another note, you also had the haters who were staring from a distance, wishing to be in their shoes.

B.G. and his boys were going in. They were dropping straight gangsta shit, song after song. B.G. turned that shit the fuck out! He even had two butt naked strippers on stage, eating each other out while pouring V.S.O.P Remy all over themselves. The Voodoo Lounge was off glass tonight. This shit didn't make sense; it was too lit!

This nigga B.G. was putting on for the real niggas in the building. He showed love to all the gangstas and thugs. Once he got off stage, he came and vibed with K-Dog and the rest of the Takeover crew. Everybody was vibing up in that bitch. It wasn't even funny. Whatever could come to your head and you could imagine on some gangsta shit, that's exactly what happened.

People were still vibing inside the building and outside in the parking lot all the way until the club closed. Well, at least until Precious and ole boy walked past. Without thinking twice, K-Dog reached out and grabbed Precious by the arm.

"Boy, why the fuck you grabbing me by my dam arm like you fucking crazy or something?" K-Dog knew Precious was white girl wasted because she knew better than talking to him like that.

"So, this how you doin' my nigga?" K-Dog asked while looking at her like she was the dirt on the bottom of his new shoes.

"Fuck you talking 'bout? Ain't nobody told Killa to get his self locked up! I been told that nigga to get out the fuckin game!" she snapped. Then continued, "So, if a bitch wanna have fun and do them, then oh, muthafuckin' well. It is what it is," she said, twisting her neck like a ghetto bitch out the projects.

Meanwhile, while K-Dog and Precious were having a little heart to heart moment. Lil' Coon eased up behind ole boy out the blue and punched him dead in his chin, knockin' him clean out! Buddy boy fell so hard, then Coon went to kicking him and stomping on his face.

"Maaannn, fuck this shit!" Lil' Coon pulled out his 9 mm handgun and shot him in the chest four times before everyone jumped in their vehicles and pulled off. They left ole boy there for dead, bleeding out on the sidewalk. Twenty minutes after, while K-Dog was heading up Sistrunk, he noticed a car following behind him. K-Dog turned into 1stop gas station and jumped out with his A.R. 15 in his hand. Just as the vehicle turned in to 1stop, K-Dog cocked his choppa back, putting a 7.62 in the head as he waited. To his surprise it was Bray who pulled up and got out.

"Boy, what you doing with that big ass gun like you fena go to war or something?" Bray asked, walking up.

"Girl, what the fuck you doing following me?" K-Dog said as he opened the back door of his Rover and placing the stick back inside.

"Boy, you is real paranoid, ain't nobody following you. I was already headed in this direction, then I saw you. Killa wanted me to holla at you about something."

"Well, I'm listening." K-Dog leaned on the back of the SUV while looking straight into her eyes. Bray thought about how she was gonna let it out.

"Umm… I got a plan that will get Killa outta jail, but it will take a lot of time and plottin'," she said.

"Okay and?" K-Dog said.

"I'ma have to go undercover as an agent if I wanna pull this off."

"You talking 'bout working as a C.I.? Hell naw, girl we don't rock like that!" K-Dog said, after kissing his teeth.

"No, no, no… man! It ain't what you thinking 'bout, boy. I don't even much play like that." Bray was referring to Queen's situation. "I'll tell you what... follow behind me, and I'll tell you everything okay."

"Aight," he said and they both jumped in their cars and pulled off.

Stepping Up
11:47 a.m.
Lil' Coon
CHAPTER 20

Ever since Lil' Coon became the man on the streets, he no longer had to be on the block all day serving. All he really had to do now was pick up and drop off. The money was coming so fast, it made it hard for Coon to fold it. In less than nine months, he was able to buy that drop top Bentley coupe straight off the showroom floor. The car even came with a blunt in it. However, he wasn't about to smoke some shit he ain't roll. Although he was making big dollars, he still had to ride around strapped because of all the haters. The fact that he was breaking bread and looking out didn't matter because people still hated. In Lauderdale, sometimes they hated you even more for that.

Lil' Coon had two dudes in all-black approach him while doing a pickup and drop off. He felt something wasn't right because they had their hoodies on and were walking behind him at a fast pace. As he opened the door to his new Bentley, Coon drew his gun, catching the niggas off guard.

119

"Y'all looking for a sweet lick, but this the wrong place, man. Now get the fuck on the ground before I blow y'all fucking chests out ya fuckin backs," said Coon. Both men got on the ground like they were told. Once they laid down, he took their guns from their waistbands, disarming them. Instead off killing them on spot, Lil' Coon had other plans for them. He pulled out his phone and made a call. In less than ten minutes, a white van with sliding doors pulled up. Four guys with ski masks jumped out and duct taped both dudes before throwing them back into the vehicle and pulling off into the night air.

The next morning, Lil' Coon was laying in bed next to Myesha, smoking a blunt when his phone rung.

"Hello?"

"Aye bruh, turn the TV on Channel 7, right now."

"Yeah, fool, aight. I got you," Coon responded. Grabbing the remote control, hitting the power the button, he turned the 72-inch smart flat screen on, putting it on Channel 7 News.

"Hi, my name is Shakita Cooks. And we are live on 27th Ave and 9th St in Washington Park. And what we have is a deadly devastating tragedy, and right behind me is where two young black males around the ages of eighteen to twenty. Both were beaten badly and hung naked. From my understanding if I'm not mistaken, this incident is related to a drug gang. Whoever the killer or killers were, they left powerful message." The reporter stepped to the side, letting the camera man zoom in.

"We don't know how they got here or how long they been here, but we do know it was no longer then six hours ago. We will update you when the authorities give more information. Thank you. Coming to you live at Channel 7 News." Lil' Coon smiled at himself as he turned off the

T.V. Reaching under the cover, he felt on Myesha.

"Let me get sum." It seemed like killing was something that got Lil' Coon off. It aroused him every time a life was taken.

***

Two Days Later
10:38 p.m.

Lil' Coon decided to hit the gentleman's club in Pompano Beach off Dixie and Atlantic, called Flava. As he pulled up in the parking lot, in his drop top Bentley, all eyes were on him. Lil' Coon parked in the V.I.P. section and got out.

Nobody had an idea that Lil' Coon had his shooters posted fifty yards away, just waiting for anything to pop off. Lil' Coon was sharp as a razor went it came to this street shit, and plus, he knew niggas was trying to jack him, so of course, he had his shooters/gunman's camouflaging in the cut.

Lil' Coon got out, wearing an all-black Coogi fit with a chain that was too big, and of course, you know he was strap with his Glock 40. Like a boss, he walked right in without paying or getting patted down. Once entering the stripe club, he made his way towards the bar.

"Hey, Coon! What can I do or get you tonight?" the bartender said, hoping to get a few dollars out of him.

"Let me get a bottle of Remy V.S.O.P. and four bottles of water." Lil' Coon pulled out a wad of blue hundred-dollar bills.

"And, $5,000 worth of ones." He handed her the money and waited until she gave him what he paid for. Once he received his things, he walked towards the stage. There was an area reserved for him right in front. He placed the bucket with the bottle in it and the wads of ones on the table.

All the money hungry bitches flocked over him as if they were flies to shit. They came from left and right continuously, but Coon rejected them one at a time. The weed aroma was now in the air and the bottles were popped. Lil' Coon chilled alone at his table until he saw a bad bitch pass by. She had a figure like Buffy Da Body. He grabbed her by the wrist politely and placed her in his lap. She knew he was a big dog from the time he entered the building, so she accepted. She was watching him the entire time while he declined every stripper that came on to him. The fact that he grabbed hold of her made her feel special because that meant he chose her over all the others.

She wasted no time dancing for him. They didn't speak, though. She just danced while he threw money and watched it fall from the sky. There were those niggas that stood on the sideline, mean mugging Lil' Coon. If looks could've killed Lil' Coon would've died hours ago.

Finally, the alcohol and weed started to kick in. especially when Plies "I Am the Club" came on. That's when Coon started to really feel himself. If these niggas wanted to hate, then he was now giving them a reason to do so. He threw money like he had a money tree. But it fell fast like it was coming from one of those money guns.

Lil' Coon wanted an exclusive dance, so he took lil' mama to the private section where anything goes. If the price was right and your money was right, then it was all game. Lil' Coon paid the guard who was standing at the entrance $150 before walking inside. Coon still had his bottle in his hand as they both entered a booth that was the size of a prison cell. Out the gate. she asked for $250, which wasn't a problem. After she received her money, she proceeded to take off her clothes. She wasn't wearing anything but a thong and some net stockings anyway, so it didn't take long.

Then she began unbuckling Lil' Coon's pants and pulled out his dick. The oral performance she put on him was the best he ever experienced thus far. She worked her magic for a consistent ten minutes, using both hands. She also used her mouth for the sucking. Her head game was on point and even though he wasn't a headhunter, he enjoyed every minute of it.

How he was at the point where he wanted to beat her guts up, so he made her put a rubber on him. She put it on without using any hands, then straddled him while being topless. Baby had to ease down on his big dick, but once she got used to the size, she started bouncing up and down on him like she lost her damn mind. She rode him like a pony as she got in her zone. Then, she began screaming out of pleasure as he started to dick her down.

"Ooooohhh, shit! I'm about to cum, baby," she said as she started grinding harder and rotating her hips, getting him all the way up inside her. Within thirty seconds, she jumped up and started rubbing her clit until she started squirting everywhere. She did this about four times. After she got herself off, she wanted Lil' Coon to hit her from the back. But for some reason, he couldn't bust a nut for shit. It's now been like thirty minutes and he still couldn't bust.

"Boy, you ain't nut yet?" the stripper asked him while he was still long stroking her from the back. He was even hitting the bottom of her ocean.

"Naw, not yet, shawty," he responded, wiping the sweat from his brows with his forearm.

"Hold up for a minute, boy, because this don't make no damn sense," she said, pulling his dick out of her and sticking it in her ass. He never fucked a chick in her ass before, but I guess tonight would be his first time. Her anus became so wet that it was hard for him to stay inside. It kept slipping out as he tried to bust her ass up. He never knew an ass could get wetter than a pussy, and that turned him on even more.

Just as he was at the peak of busting a nut, something that he was trying to do a long time ago, he started smelling shit. He was fucking her in the ass so hard she couldn't hold her mud. She was trying to tell him to stop, but he wasn't listening. He was too busy trying to bust his nut. When he realized that she was shitting on him, he still didn't stop. He had to get his. A couple minutes later. he came harder than he ever did but he was also, 38 hot because he couldn't believe she shitted on him. She felt so bad that after she cleaned herself up, she gave him back his money and exited the room.

***

Usually, the club wouldn't allow anyone to leave with a cup of liquor in their hand, let alone a bottle, but since it was Lil' Coon, he got a g-pass. As he approached his Bentley, he felt the alcohol take full effect. However, he knew how to handle himself and get himself back right. Believe it or not, he leaned on the back of his vehicle and place his fingers down his throat, allowing the alcohol to come back up in a rush.

In the process of getting himself together, he got another one of those vibes that told him something was not right. Before he could do anything, he looked up and found himself staring down the barrel of a gun.

"Yeah, bitch ass nigga! Caught yo' ass slippin'. Let me get all dis shit," one of the gunmen said as he took Lil' Coon's chain. "And while you at, empty them pockets too fuck nigga."

Just as Coon was going for his gun, the other man hit him upside the head with the butt of his gun, knocking him down. They were so focused on Coon; they didn't realize that his hitters were creeping up behind them with AK's until it was too late. They ended up being the ones that were ambushed. Lil' Coon's men had them swiss cheesed and left them lying in a puddle of blood.

Every Thug Needs A Good Woman
Killa
CHAPTER 21

K illa had been transferred from county jail to the federal penitentiary in California months ago. As far as doing time, it was sweet but when it came to the inmates that's where it got deadly. Niggas from all over the U.S. were there doing time, so if you weren't a gang member or a nigga with status, then you had it bad.

There was plenty money being generated on the compound by the inmates and officers. Drugs were available as well, and lots of it. This is where most of the money came from. If you were incarcerated in one of these federal prisons, you had to be on point 24/7 because at any given moment anything was liable to pop off. Especially, in the California Federal Penitentiary.

Killa had kicked Precious to the curb like a bad habit. To him, she was now not worth anything more than some old dirty laundry. Everything he had given her; he somehow found a way to take back. This left her broke and homeless. Killa was doing his thing up in there. He had officers on his team, bringing him in cell phones, drugs, and anything else he could want.

One weekend while Killa was inside his cell, getting ready for visitation, a female officer entered his room. She wanted him to fuck her brains out before going to visitation. He already knew that, though, because he had been fucking her on a regular and every time she wanted more.

"Meka, not right now," he said. "I gotta get ready for an important meeting with my girl." He continued to get ready like she wasn't standing in his way.

"Boy, I don't care about that. I want some dick, and I want some now!" she said, walking up to him and reaching for his pants.

"You can't wait until a nigga get back?" he said, getting irritated with her. He was starting to lose his patience, but it wasn't nothing he could do about it because he created the monster that was inside her. If she couldn't get what she wanted, she would threaten him with locking him down in confinement. That what made him give in and just fuck her from the back, so she didn't see how pissed he was in his face.

Killa was late when he walked into the visitation room. Bray had already been waiting for him a little less than an hour and a half. He walked up to her and gave her a big hug while kissing her down as if he wasn't just fucking the C.O. bitch Meka. Bray's whole plan was to go undercover to expose all the corrupted members of the government. Mainly those who were distributing tons of cocaine.

The very moment they sat down, the two of them got down to business. They went over the plan on how they were going to bring the crooked government members down. Bray knew they were responsible for her boo being locked away, along with many others. That's why she took it upon herself to do what she was doing. Well, at least, that was one of the reasons. The other one was that she was truly in love with Killa. And Killa respected the fact that she would go the extra mile for him.

Bray was the definition of a real ride or die chick. She was loyal as hell on all grounds. Even though Killa had everything he could dream of, she still went out her way to make sure he didn't lack for nothing.

After they got finished going through the plays, they took pictures and ate until they were both full. But to put the icing on the cake, they snuck into the restroom and got a little quickie in. By the time they knew it, visitation was over. The three o'clock shift had come in, but it seemed like they both just got there.

"Visitation is now over!" announced an officer over the megaphone. After Killa and Bray embraced each other, they went their separate ways.

"Bye, boo!" Bray yelled as she was walking out the door.

***

Later that night, Killa walked out the quad and went inside the officer control booth where the two female officers were. When Killa entered, the two were vibing, listening to Plies.

"Wuz up, Ms. King?" Killa said.

"Nothing, tired as hell, and waiting for this dam shift to be over, so I can take my ass home," she responded.

There was a box of Popeyes chicken sitting on the desk in front of her.

"Hey, Killa, what you got going on, boy?" asked Ms. King's co-worker, with her dick junkie ass.

"Shit! I just came to holla at Ms. King, hoping she'd give me some of that Popeyes she got up there."

Killa's mouth began to water as he watched Ms. King take a bite out of the chicken.

"Oh, you want some of this California Popeyes, huh?" said Ms. King.

"Hell yeah!" Killa said, approaching Ms. King.

"You better eat it right here too," Ms. King said, giving Killa the rest of the box of the chicken.

Killa didn't wasted no time as he devoured the remains of it within thirty seconds.

"Damn, boy, you sho can eat up sum, so I can imagine what you'd do to some pussy," the co-worker said as Killa was wiping his mouth.

"Hoe, shut up with yo' nasty ass, ain't nobody thinking about that but you," Ms. King said, shaking her head. They both knew she couldn't help herself even if she wanted to. That was the only reason she decided to work at a prison system in the first place. She didn't get the attention she was seeking on the streets, like she did with the inmates.

Master roster count had come so fast it was crazy. Everybody had to sit up in their bunks and state their names and D.C. numbers. This happened about four times a day every day of the week. After Ms. King and her co-worker came through and did count, Killa went in his stash spot and got his cell phone. Even though he was locked up, it was still as if he were a free man compared to most inmates. Not everyone was fortunate to reach out to their loved ones whenever they wanted.

As Killa hit the power button which turned on the phone, a message came in from Precious's sorry ass. Even though Killa was through with her he had to face the fact that's he was still the mother of his child. He couldn't just dismiss her like he really wanted to.

All In
March 26, 2014
K-Dog
CHAPTER 22

2½ years had flew by so quickly that it seemed like it was just yesterday when the shit went down. Javon was growing up so fast, he was already walking and talking, and Dominique was so proud. K-Dog had gotten him a pure-breaded pit bull puppy for his birthday. The dog came from a bloodline of champions.

K-Dog and Dominique had finally tied the knot. Their marriage was beautiful and the only person that was missing was his best man Killa. K-Dog took her to the Virgin Islands for their honeymoon. The whole time, they completely enjoyed each other's company. They did the whole nine, which included, scuba diving, jet skiing, sky diving, and swimming with the dolphins. Most of all, they enjoyed the food.

Dominique was intrigued by how much Killa had matured from the person who spent most his life in the streets, to the man that was now invested in her life. They were young, rich, and most importantly, happy. Not only that, but they gave back to their community a great deal. Dominique had gotten into the real estate business. She was phenomenal at buying houses and flipping them. It was something she wanted to do for a long time. And K-Dog made it happen for her.

While Killa was locked up, serving that life sentence, K-Dog and Lil' Coon made sure that he was straight, along with Lil' Coon who was still doing things that were illegal. The both of them were playing a major role in Bray's plan to help Killa get out of jail.

Today was the day for K-Dog and Lil' Coon to purchase a large lump sum of pure cocaine from the Secretary of State. The question was, how in the hell was Bray gonna pull something like this off? Let's just say a woman would go to hell and back for the man she truly loves.

The plan was for the three of them to meet up with the Secretary of State, who was a big distributor when it came down to the underworld. The meeting was taking place at the Secretary's mansion in Washington D.C.

Bray had to first sank her nails into the Secretary flesh, by simply seducing him in ways only a woman who's determine enough to go all out, even if her life was on the line.

It was like taking candy from a baby because after the second encounter, Bray had with the target, she was on the road with K=Dog and Lil' Coon.

***

Tuesday...
4:26am
For two whole days, Bray, K-Dog, and Lil' Coon, had driven from Fort Lauderdale to Washington D.C., they were dressed as business individuals with $1.5 million stashed in the trunk of their rental without being pulled

by any law enforcers. The three of them made it safe and sound to their designation.

With over $1.5 million and a plan that may cost them their lives if it doesn't well, the three of them entered Washington D.C. and rented separate hotel rooms at the Marriott. They even stayed for an additional three days just making sure that everyone was on the same page

On the third day, Bray got up early that morning and began fixing herself up, preparing to go to the mansion, which was owned by Robert Bertoz, the Secretary of State. Everything was now in motion. The only thing left to be done was for Lil' Coon and K-Dog to sit back and wait for Bray's phone call which would give them the green light for them to go.

In the meantime, the two of them kicked back, blew a few trees, ate some breakfast, and talked about their other half as they waited. A few hours went by and K-Dog and Lil' Coon began to grow impatient because they still didn't receive the call. Just then, K-Dog's phone finally rang out the blue.

"Hello?"

"We in," Bray said, giving him the green light before disconnecting the call.

"Let's ride, lil' homie," K-Dog said, standing up and walking towards the front door.

Within thirty minutes, K-Dog and Lil' Coon pulled up to the mansion that belonged to the Secretary of State. Two security guards were standing out front with a couple of highly trained German shepherds. They had M-P5 assault rifles strapped around their shoulders as well. These weren't the type of security officers they had in the hood.

Both security guards approached the vehicle as K-Dog pulled up. K-Dog rolled down the driver's side window and gave them the code. In no time, they were able to gain entrance. Another pair of guards were already waiting for them to pull up after they've already entered. The guards patted them down thoroughly after they exited the vehicle. K-Dog and Lil' Coon walked to the trunk of the rental and grabbed four duffle bags filled with 100-dollar bills.

Bray was laying next to the head boss in a swimsuit when K-Dog and Coon stepped in the back where the pool area was. The sun was bright, and the weather was nice out. All that was left to do now was exchange the money for the drugs. When Bray saw their faces, she knew it was game time. As soon as she saw them, she put on her game face and got straight down to business.

"I'm so glad you were able to make it, Kenny. How are you?" Bray said, jumping up to greet him.

"I'm taking it one day at a time."

"That's good. Now will you both please follow me. I would like to introduce you to a friend of mine. Mr. Bertoz, please meet Kenny and Tommy," she said. Then Bray extended her arm towards K-Dog and Lil' Coon. Mr. Bertoz got up from his lawn chair, wearing only a pair of long black dress pants.

"Fellows, fellows, fellows, nice to meet you," he said, shaking their hands one at a time. He looked deep into their eyes while doing so. Mr. Bertoz only engaged to do business with them off the strength of Bray anyway. It was a favor for a favor kind of thing. Being the type of person, he was, a money hungry animal, he got straight to the point. As fast as he could hurry this process up to get them to leave, the faster he could get back to Bray.

"So, lets get down to business," Bertoz said, kicking the small talk to the side. Then, he walked over to the front of a long glass table and stood next to a pile of kilos. Bray had her mini mic and recorder attached to her two-piece swimsuit. They were positioned dead in Bertoz direction.

"Is it all there?" Bertoz asked.

"All 1.5 mill," K-Dog said, placing the duffle bags on the glass table, before signaling for Lil' Coon to do the same. "Now the question is, is er'thang in there, and I'm talking about ALL 1.5 million worth of that cocaine?" K-Dog said, staring Bertoz down.

"Of course, it is my friend." Bertoz burst out laughing. But, while he enjoyed his laughter, the fat that clung to his body was giggling. It looked like a giant sea lion with a lot of rolls. It was such an ugly sight to see. Lil' Coon skinned his face up in disgust, but he said nothing.

K-Dog and Lil' Coon reviewed the large number of drugs while Mr. Bertoz security guards ran the cash through the money counting machines.

Beep! The money machine sounded as the last bundle of cash was accounted for.

"1.5 million, boss! All of it is there," one of the guards said, looking up to Bertoz from the machine. 2 ½ hours had gone by before K-Dog and Lil' Coon had to wait until they were able to walk away.

"Ok, fellows, nice doing business with you," Mr. Bertoz said as he walked to where Bray was and wrapped his fat arm around her neck, before trying to slide his nasty ass tongue down her throat. Now it was over, and they were one step away from getting Killa out of the feds.

***

A month later, after they sealed the deal with one of the most powerful and corrupt persons' in the white house. K-Dog and Lil' Coon took Dominique and Myesha on a yacht-style ride. K-Dog had just bought it, so they celebrated by eating lobster tails they caught themselves. You know, that real playa shit that be going on when a nigga emerges from rags to riches. Truth be told K-Dog was the founder of the Take Over Empire. Although, it was no longer his hands being dirty, he was still and will always be a member regardless.

Dominique and Myesha laid in their bikinis on the top deck, drinking champagne. In the meantime, Coon and K-Dog went to the lower deck to discuss business. Finally, as they arrived back to land, K-Dog pulled the yacht over to the side of the wall that separated the brackish water from his backyard, then tied it up. Lil' Coon had a duffle bag that contained seventeen kilos and $300,000. Exiting the yacht, he walked straight to his S.R.T. 8 Dodge Charger and put the duffle bag into his trunk.

Once Lil' Coon secured the bags, he and Myesha got into the car and went their separate way from the others. Dominique made sure the coast was clear before climbing into the jacuzzi but naked. She lit candles and placed them all around the outer edges of the hot tub. The night air was just right, it wasn't too humid or too breezy for her. Not even five minutes later, K-Dog came out through the sliding glass door to join her. He also was wearing absolutely nothing.

Dominique didn't even give him time to get all the way in before straddling him. She kissed him passionately as she grabbed his wood. "Damn, baby, you hard as a rock," she said, while arching her back and easing his manhood inside of her. K-Dog had to brace himself before fully entering her. He wanted to make sure he went to work and gave her everything she wanted. As he straight pounded her pussy, water began splashing everywhere. Dominique loved it when he took control. Once he took over, she became totally submissive under the touch of his spell. She loved every moment of it.

In about twenty minutes, she was on the verge of climaxing. "Baby, I'm fena cum. Ooohhh, gosh!" she said while shifting gears on him. She started rotating her hips and grinding harder.

"I'm cumming too, bae," K-Dog said, gripping her tightly and fucking her faster and harder.

"I'm cumming, baby!" Dominique started screaming and grabbing the back of K-Dogs neck with one hand. With the other, she held tightly onto the edge of jacuzzi as she began to bounce up and down on him, until she shook out of control. They both climaxed together.

K-Dog froze up when he bust his nut. He grabbed Dominique around the waist, trying to make her stop, but she kept going. "Is this how you want it, daddy?" she asked while still going, causing K-Dog's eyes to roll to the back of his head.

"Oooh, shit! Damn, girl, what you doing to me?" he said. Dominique was still bouncing up and down on him and biting on her bottom lip. She rode him until she couldn't no more. But that still didn't stop her from going down on him and getting him right back up.

"Baby are you ready for round two?" she asked him as she climbed back on top.

"Oh, my fuckin' gawd girl! What you really tryna do, kill me?" K-Dog asked.

Love is Pain
Lil' Coon
CHAPTER 23

Sunday morning the 1Stop was on swole. It was jammed packed with dope boys and go getters. Everyone was showing off their vehicles, especially if it had big rims and candy paint jobs. Hustlers from all over Broward County came out to post up and watch the car show that the 1Stop kept at the corner of Sistrunk Blvd and 27th Ave. All the "get money" crews were out there too. You had the Y.G. hustlers, Snap Money Gang, F.B.G. known as the Free Band Gang, the G.M.B.'s aka Get Money Babii crew, and more. All of them were either hustlers or check boys. Either way, they got dumb cash on a daily.

Then you had the Take Over team who was on set as well. Each member of Take Over was ballin' out and stuntin' out of control. 1Stop was the place to be on Sunday's for the ones who didn't attend church services. Some people even went to church and came there after to chill with other people that actually got money. Bitches dressed in the latest designer just to walk around in. In addition, there was a dice game going on every corner surrounding it.

Lil' Coon, who now possessed full control of Take

Over, and his team were standing around their vehicles with the trunk popped. All members had rifles with them also, just in case a nigga decided to get loco. They had things that would get theirs mind right, asap!

Bottles of Remy V.S.O.P was stacked on top of one another in water coolers, grade aroma was roaming all through the air, and Lil' Coon was standing on top of his Bentley without a shirt on, acting a straight fool, with two bottles in each hand. While he was getting attention, a '73 donk that sat on 28's and candy apple red, with a drop top that showed off the matching interior, came through blasting some Soulja Slim. When Lil' Coon noticed who it was, he jumped off the top of the Bentley and grabbed his AR-15 out of his trunk. Very politely, he cocked it back, putting a 7.62 in the chamber as he walked towards the donk. Once he'd reached the car, he pointed his weapon at the side of it while releasing fire. He shot at it until he completely knocked out the motor.

"Nigga, you think shit sweet round here?" Coon said as he ran up on the man who was driving, pointing the stick directly at his head.

"Aight, dawg, aiight damn! I gotcha bro," dude said, covering his head.

"Fuck Dat! Matter fact, nigga get out before I blast yo' fuck ass."

Lil' Coon snatched open the door and dragged buddy out of his car by his throat, throwing him on the ground.

"Sleep check this nigga," Lil' Coon said to his right-hand man.

Sleep searched him only to find a 357. Magnum that was on his waist, before running his hands through buddy pockets, taking all the money. Lil' Coon violated the man like he was a bitch. But, to make matters worse, what he instructed next was just foul.

"Sleep, throw hits in the air and make it rain," he said as if dude was some cheap hoe in a strip club. All the bitches started running over to where the money was falling. 100-dollar bills, 50-dollar bills, 20's all the way down to 5-dollar bills were scattered everywhere. And the females collected the cash out the air before it even hit the ground like savages.

The niggas who knew or knew of Lil' Coon knew he was trigger happy. Busting a cap in your ass was something he lived for. It wasn't anything new. He didn't even understand why buddy even tried it. However, BSO came and shut everything down within twenty minutes after that. The Broward Sheriff's Office were the nastiest cops ever, so when they jumped out, people wasted no time hailing ass.

Later on, that evening, both Coon and Sleep decided they should hit the block. Sure enough, there was a big dice game going on. It didn't matter what the time of day was. You were guaranteed to find a dice game going on in every hood. Lauderdale was a place where hustlers and head busters emerged from fraud, selling drugs, boosting, burglaries, robberies, and anything else u can name. You always had to be on point because if caught slipping, that's your ass. A nigga or bitch would fast talk you out of anything quick!

Lil' Coon and Sleep came out of the Bentley wearing all black as they approached the group of young hustlers. Don't get it twisted, niggas knew Sleep as well. They knew he wasn't nothing nice. When the group of men shooting dice saw Sleep walking in their direction, they began to feel some type of way because they never knew what to expect from this crazy ass nigga.

"Damn, Lil' Coon we don't want no problems bruh. We just tryna make a little money bruh. We've got mouths to feed too," one of the dudes said.

"If y'all niggas don't start cheatin and shit, then we ain't gonna have no problems," Lil' Coon said pulling out a stack of blue faces.

***

Two Days Later

Lil' Coon was in Parkway, chilling at this chick named Jazz house. Jazz was a bad bitch who got gwap off doing fraud. She was definitely a little snack. She was 5'5," 138 pounds. red bone with long hair. She had her own house that was paid for, with cash, and about three foreign whips. She did her thang no doubt. Jazz also did taxes and used that business to wash all her illegal money she made.

Coon had a thing for Jazz because she was always about her issue. She was a straight up go-getting money bitch. And if you weren't on her level, then she gave you no type of play. Bitches from Lauderdale always got the big head when they started making bread. That's just how it went. Somehow, Jazz was different, though. If she knew you had potential, she'd look out.

If you wanted to make money and get on your feet, Jazz was the person you'd go see. A lot of niggas was working for her. She was the one you'd call if you wanted a rental, or hotel, or whatever else that could be paid with a credit or debit card. She had numbers all day and gave you the best deal you'd find. Or even, if you were more into robbing or whatever. She'd give you a poker to go bust a bitch window out with.

If that was the case, in return, all you had to do was bring her whatever information you got out of the pocketbooks. She wanted it all; credit cards, bank cards, check books, I.D.'s, socials, and licenses. Mostly white women were her target, though. However, one thing about Jazz was that she was crazy about Lil' Coon. Anything he asked her for, she made it happen. Even though she was older than Coon was, in her eyes, it didn't matter because she was on that Pretty Ricky "Age Ain't Nothing but A Number" type of mentality. It didn't help that she also loved that song and played the hell out of it when he was around.

Lil' Coon was chilling, smoking loud, while Jazz was doing her one-two, emptying out people's accounts and shit. Then transferring the funds into a John Doe account. Once she was done, Jazz grabbed her Gucci pocketbook and filled it with the credit cards that she'd just loaded. Jazz turned towards Lil' Coon and said.

"Bae, lets go get something to eat, I'm hungry," she said. The sound of food put a smile on his face.

"Let's go!" he said, jumping up, grabbing his car keys.

***

Myesha had a funny feeling that Lil' Coon was sleeping around on her with other bitches, but as bad as she wanted to find out even if it broke her heart. Myesha had to do what she had to do.

Lil' Coon jumped into Jazz's Range Rover, leaving his vehicle parked into Jazz garage. Myesha was parked down the street in a rental, watching them from a distance.

As Jazz pulled out of her driveway and headed towards Myesha who got low, jumping behind them.

Myesha just knew that something wasn't right, though, but she couldn't place her finger on it, so today was the day that she would get to the bottom of it. The entire time she followed them, she started to let her thought get the best of her. After all, how could Coon do this to her after everything she'd sacrificed. Tears began to fall from her eyes as she pulled into the parking lot, she had seen them turn into. She waited for them to get out the car and go into the restaurant.

Coon and Jazz got out the vehicle, walking hand in hand, which confirmed everything Myesha wanted to know. "The infidelity," she yelled as she slammed her balled up fists against the steering wheel. Myesha must've forgotten that her and Coon weren't even married, but it was obvious he didn't even care.

Lil' Coon was sitting at the table, enjoying Jazz's company. He didn't know that all along Myesha was watching. Jazz knew Coon was in a relationship, but that did not stop her from being a friend to him. She respected his situation, but she also didn't mind because a woman of her caliber knew how to play her position.

While they ate and enjoyed small talk, Myesha entered the restaurant. It wasn't long before she found where they were seated and strolled herself down the aisle towards them. When Lil' Coon looked up, he saw Myesha, standing there crying with pure evil and hatred in her eyes.

"Bae, what's up, what you doing here?" Coon said, looking surprised.

"Don't fucking 'bae' me, who is this bitch?" Myesha asked while pointing in Jazz's direction.

"Bitch?" Jazz repeated as she got up.

"Yeah, you heard me, …. BITCH!" Myesha said again. Luckily, Jazz wasn't in any mood to go back and forth with no female about a nigga. She had more important things to worry about.

"Listen, girl," Jazz said in irritated voice. "I don't have time for that childish ass shit you on. I've got other things to focus on then to be arguing with some stalker bitch. Get your shit together boo-boo," Jazz said as she grabbed her purse and walked off.

"Aye! Coon don't worry about the bill I'll take care of it. You know where to find me if you want me. By the way, it's Ms. Boss Bitch to you," Jazz said over her shoulder while she was about to exit.

Even though the beef wasn't between them, Myesha was willing to take it all the way there about her man. However, Jazz was way too classy to fight over some dick. Especially, when she knew she could have it anytime she wanted. She left Myesha standing there, looking like a damn fool. Most of all baby was fuming inside from the depths of her soul.

"Who was she? and don't lie!" Myesha demanded Lil' Coon.

Back to the Streets
January 18th
Killa
CHAPTER 24

It was time for Killa to walk back into freedom after a long 3 ½ years. That's right! He was getting an emergency release. It was all thanks to Bray, after she was able to pull off blackmailing of Robert Bertoz. Bray was going to expose his dirt to the public and ruin his life completely. Instead, she mad Robert a deal. All he had to do was pull a few strings to her man out of the Feds. He agreed in an instant, but only on one condition, she had to turn in everything she had on him. Which of course, after making a copy, she agreed just in case, he wasn't a man of his word.

As Killa and Bray headed to his spot from the airport, he was still in the blind of the surprise party they were throwing for him. As Bray pulled into his driveway, they both got out of the car and entered the house. Once Killa, stepped in and turned the lights on. Everyone yelled, "SURPRIIISSEEE. Welcome home!" He couldn't believe his eyes. Once again, he was caught off guard only this time it was a good thing.

"Waz up, boy?" K-Dog said, walking up to greet his best friend. Then, he stepped to the side to let the other Take Over members embrace him. They had a blast partying until four o'clock in the morning. Killa was so fucked up that after everyone left and Bray had to help get him in bed. He hadn't drunk so much alcohol in a while.

"Damn, bae! I'm fucked up," Killa said as Bray laid next to him.

"I told yo' butt to take it easy, but nahhhh, you had to go hard," Bray said before she kissed him on his forehead. "Now look at ya, poor baby. Had you would've listened to me you would've been able to get some," she continued while taunting him.

Killa sat up quickly and said, "I'm fucked up, but I ain't dead," with a slur.

"Boy! You ain't in no condition to give me what I want right na," she teased.

"Girl, don't ever underestimate the power that I'm possessed with, now come here," Killa said as he reached over and pulled Bray on top of him.

"Stop it, baby! You not ready for all this," Bray said, laughing, but not giving in to her words.

Killa responded by saying, "Take this shit off and let's get down to business."

Bray didn't waste any time stripping down to absolutely nothing. Once she was fully naked, she looked over to Killa and said, "Now, shall we?"

***

After spending 3 ½ years in the Feds, Killa decided it was best for him to let the dope game go because what he learned while incarcerated was far better. Plus, he had less chances of going back. It was impossible for any individual that was raised in the streets all his life to turn away from a life of crime. Although, that same path is where he received his PhD, but at the same time, while he was incarcerated, Killa became spiritually enlightened.

Killa knew that in order to for him to travel on the path that leads to the light with the secret society, he must first turn away from all paths that lead to destruction. One must first, be worthy to have favor to receive grace. And this grace was a gift from God but on a higher degree. The freemason's is a fraternity known for Brotherhood, laws to travel on this path consists of living righteous in all ye doings.

Bray was so amazed to see Killa, giving up the life of crimes. All that prison talk about changing his life had finally came to past. Y'all know how it goes, every time a nigga gets locked up the first thing, they say is that they're a changed man. Then as soon as they get released, they go back to the same lifestyle that got them caught up before.

Killa decided to invite K-Dog and the rest of the crew over to his house for some special announcement he was about to make. The house was packed with family and friends when he entered the living room. Everyone was having small talk about this, that and the third until he came in wearing all-white. He looked around at the assembly of guests before saying, "Praise Yahweh!" while spreading his hands towards the sky. "It's a blessing to be here today. I give thanks to the father for making this possible because without him, I would've still been on the road of destruction, but by his grace and I was able to receive favor," he continued. Then he walked up to Bray and touched the side of her face.

Killa then turned and faced Bray and said, "Without you being in my life and sticking by my side, I don't know where I would've been. You believed in me and saw something that I didn't even see in myself. From my heart to the depths of my soul, I want to say thank you for bringing out the best in me baby." Killa got down and kneeled on one knee, pulling out a black box from his pockets. Then he looked deep into Bray's eyes and asked, "Will you marry me and explore the world with me?"

Bray was in a state of shock when Killa opened the box and pulled out a 6-karat diamond ring and placed it on her finger. "Oh baby, I can't believe this is happening," she said. Bray became so overwhelmed with excitement that tears began to fall from her eyes.

"So, what do you say?" Killa asked with a pause.

"Yes, baby, of course, I do!" Bray responded.

Afterwards, Bray gave her vows and Killa kissed her with such a passionate kiss that everyone started clapping. There must be a God out there somewhere that's making this all possible. Another black brother that made it from the bottom to the top in one piece. To be honest, a lot of guys from the ghetto that chose to live a dope boy lifestyle didn't ever make it out alive. However, this was a prime example that if an individual decides to hang up his gloves and leave the game alone, then better days would come.

Lil' Coon was standing in the corner, kicking it with his right-hand man, Sleep. The whole time he had his eyes on this pretty young thang that was also watching him as well. Bray happened to notice her best friend, checking him out and intervened by saying, "That's Lil' Coon. He's K-Dog and Yashua people."

"Girrrrllll, he is so fine," she responded.

"Lil' Coon is straight. He's good peoples. That man is loyal to the core, he's one of the reasons why my boo is home," Bray said, looking in the direction of where Coon was standing.

"Well, does he have peoples, Bray?" her friend asked.

"To be honest, girl, I don't know what he has going on. All I can say is he's a good nigga," Bray lied, trying not to throw salt on his name.

"Girl, I ain't gonna lie, I want his fine ass."

Nightmares Come True
K-Dog
CHAPTER 25

K-Dog was sitting in his office at the car wash with Lil' Coon and Sleep, talking about business plans. Sleep wanted a Lamborghini for his birthday, so that's why they were at the lot instead of running the streets. While K-Dog was making a call to put in the order for Sleep's Lambo. Lil' Coon and Sleep made small talk.

"Aye, Coon! Whatever happened to that lil pretty thang you met at Killa's house?" Sleep asked.

"Oh, you talking about Shawn? She good, bruh," he replied. "She hit me up from time to time." Coon said.

"You got them draws yet, my boy?" Sleep asked without hesitation.

"What?"

"Nigga you heard me," Sleep said, laughing.

"Well, you know I can't tell you that," said Coon.

"Why?"

"Because it's a secret!" Now Lil' Coon was the one laughing.

"Yeah, whatever, nigga," Sleep said, looking over at K-Dog.

K-Dog hung up the phone and said, "Okay, love birds everything is taken care of. The Lam should be in next month with all the paperwork."

"That's what I'm talking about baby!" Sleep said excitedly while rubbing his hands together.

At around 9:12 p.m. both Sleep and Lil' Coon had to go check up on some money by some lil' niggas from Dixie Court. As Lil' Coon and Sleep stood up to leave, Coon looked over to -K-Dog, dapping him up and said, "We out, big homie."

"Aight, gangstas, y'all be easy out there," K-Dog said as he got up and walked them out towards the exit. Then they all shook hands and departed. K-Dog and his employees were doing round checks, making sure that all the vehicles were secured before closing.

"I'll see y'all tomorrow same time, same place," K-Dog said to his employees as they went their separate ways.

One employee responded by saying, "Boss, you crazy as hell. I'll see you tomorrow." Then she walked towards her vehicle.

After K-Dog got everything squared away, he walked back into his office, sat down, and rolled a fat blunt before calling Dominique. Their conversation got so intimate that K-Dog laid back in his chair, kicking his feet up. An hour later, K-Dog ended the call, still relaxing with his eyes closed, enjoying the effects of the purple haze he just smoked. He was thinking about how he was going to do all the things that he knew Dominique craved for.

While he relaxed, a funny feeling came over him that led him to opening his eyes. To his surprise, a young kid was standing in the doorway startled him.

"Hi, can I help you?" K-Dog said, observing the kid closely.

"Yo' name K-Dog, right?" the kid asked.

"Yeah, who wanna know?" K-Dog said, taking his feet of the desk. The young kid stepped inside the office, closing the door behind him.

"You might not know who I am, but you soon fena find out," the kid said, reaching under his shirt and pulling out a 357., pointing it at K-Dog's head. "I waited a long time for this moment." the kid said, cocking the hammer back.

"WOAHH!! Hold up, hold up, young blood. Damn!" K-Dog said in a pleading manner. "You got the wrong person!"

"Naw, muthfucka, I got the right person," jit said. The kid stepped forward, getting close on K-Dog.

"Look, lil' fellow, I got money if that's what you want."

"You think this is about money? Naw, bruh it's way more than money."

"Okay, well, if it ain't about money, then what its about?" K-Dog said, looking so confused.

"THIS ABOUT MY FATHER! You killed him years ago nigga!" the kid yelled in a surprisingly strong and firm tone.

Right then it hit K-Dog like a heart attack. The same nightmares that had been haunting him came to life in a flash.

"And who is your father?" K-Dog asked, already knowing the answer.

"Pimp! You know the nigga you took away from me? See, I made a promise to kill the person that was responsible for murdering my daddy nigga." The kid had murder written all over his face.

"Listen, kid, you don't understand…" Before K-Dog was able to finish his statement, the kid shot him dead in the chest two times, knocking hm straight off his feet. Before standing over him and shooting him three more times.

"Pay back is a bitch muthafucka," the kid said, spitting on him, before turning around and leaving K-Dog to die in a puddle of blood.

***

Dominique was rushing to get to the hospital when she received a call from the authorities that said K-Dog was on his way to Plantation General Hospital. That wasn't too far away from where they lived, so about twenty minutes later, she was pulling into the hospital parking lot. Her heart was pounding irrationally. It hurt so badly she felt as if she couldn't breathe. Who could've hurt K-Dog? That was the only thing on her mind when she entered the lobby.

"Kenny Williams, he's my husband, ma'am. He just arrived not too long ago," she said to the receptionist. She didn't wait for a greeting or anything.

"One moment please…" The receptionist hit a few keys before saying… "Okay, ma'am, it says your husband is in critical condition. A doctor should be out shortly."

Dominique's head was spinning out of control. It had gotten so bad to the point that she had to take a seat because she became dizzy. She started crying and holding her stomach tight while she rocked back and forth, trying to make logic of the situation. Out of nowhere, Killa, Lil' Coon, and the rest of the crew busted in the lobby like wild bulls.

"Are you aight?" Killa asked as he picked Dominique up off the floor before she officially passed out.

"We need a doctor over here now!" Killa yelled.

Moments later, Dominique was laying in a hospital

bed with Killa by her side. Meanwhile, Lil' Coon and the others stood at attention outside of both Dominique's and K-Dog's door. The doctor had informed K-Dog's mother and Killa that Dominique was once again pregnant, and if she was planning on keeping the baby, then she shouldn't stress so much.

While Killa was sitting next to Dominique with his head down, she finally woke up.

"Where am I?" she asked Killa.

"At the hospital, how are you feelin'?" Killa asked, getting up and standing to her side.

"I feel like shit," Dominique responded as she tried to get out of bed.

"Hold up, sista soulja, you need to take it easy." Killa placed his hands on her shoulder, making her lay back down.

"No, I don't! I need to find, Kenny," Dominique argued.

"He's alright, Kenny is in a..." Killa couldn't finish his sentence.

"He's in what Killa, and don't lie to me?" Dominique demanded.

Killa explained everything to her without leaving out a single detail. K-Dog was shot five times, and Killa also informed her that she was pregnant again. Now the only question that Killa was not able to answer was the main question that everyone wanted to know the answer to. Who was the shooter? While the both of them pondered on the thought of who would want to cause K-Dog any harm, the doctor entered the room.

"How are you feeling, Ms. Williams?"

"To be honest, I don't even know," Dominique said.

"Everything is going to be alright, just relax a little bit, and I'll be discharging you in no time," the doctor said while checking her vitals, making sure everything was alright. He then explained her situation to her before walking out of the room.

Killa walked towards the window, staring out of it. He was trying so hard to figure out who was behind all of this. "Who wanted to hurt my baby?" Dominique said, breaking Killa out of his train of thought.

Killa barely could gather himself to say, "I don't know sis, but whoever…" Killa couldn't finish his sentence, his blood was bubbling over.

"Y'all just please don't do nothing crazy out there," Dominique said to Killa. But he wasn't tryna hear it. "Boy, you hear me?" Dominique asked for reassurance. She was trying her best to talk some sense into his head. "Promise me, Yashua, y'all won't spill no blood." She mentioned his attribute name for a reason. She was hoping it might soften him up, but her words fell on deaf ears.

Killa turned around, looking her dead in the eyes and said, "I can't promise you something that I know I can't keep. You got my number, so call me if you need anything." Before he left, he turned to her once more and said, "Oh, by the way somebody gonna be standing by your door 24/7, now get some sleep," with that being said, Killa walked out the room where the crew was waiting. "Find out who was the shooter, I want that muthafucka dead before sunrise!" he told the crew.

***

The Next Day

Dominique was finally being discharged upon signing the release papers. However, she couldn't just leave without seeing K-Dog for herself. Two of the Take Over crew members escorted her to K-Dog's room. While she was inside his room, the guards waited at the door. Once she was in, she walked up to where K-Dog was laying and almost fainted. She couldn't believe this bullshit. K-Dog was bandaged up everywhere, except his head. They had tubes running from his mouth as well.

Just seeing his condition made the pain for her unbearable to see. Tears began to flow again as she looked over his body. "God, help me," Dominique said to herself. Just a couple days ago, she recalled herself, making passionate love to him. No man had ever taken her places or made her feel the way K-Dog did. All kinds of thoughts started rushing through her head. Thank God, she remembered what the doctor said about not stressing too much.

After saying a prayer for K-Dog, Dominique kissed him on the forehead before walking out of his hospital room with her head held high. She was being escorted out of the hospital by the members of the Take Over, all armed. Reporters were swamping everywhere.

"Ms. Williams, could you tell me who would want to hurt your husband?" one reporter asked.

Then another one interrupted asking, "Ms. Williams, could it have been that your husband's past is finally catching up, or coming back to haunt him?"

The reporters swamped her with Ms. Williams this and Ms. Williams that. They bombarded her with questions on top of questions. With the help of the Take Over members, they finally made it to the waiting vehicle.

As they pulled off, the only thought that ran through Dominique's mind was, what was she going to do now that the love of her life was in a coma?

Mo Murder Mo Blood
Lil' Coon
11:38 p.m.
CHAPTER 26

L il' Coon was riding around with the dumbness on his mind. He and Sleep, along with the rest of the crew were strapped with automatics. Murder was the only thing on their minds, as they pulled up to the store where everybody hung out at. "Sleep, make sure you chop ery'thang down that's standin'. I want every bitch up there dead," Lil' Coon said before pulling down his ski mask and putting a 223 round in the chamber of his stick that holds 100 rounds. Once everyone was ready, they exited the vehicle in military formation. They were only four deep, but they looked like an entire army.

The blue store in Royal Palm was packed with hustlers from around the way. Not a thought came to mind as they did their thing; danger was lurking right around the corner. Lil' Coon, Sleep, and the two others crept up unseen. There were two of them on each side of the road, just in case anybody tried to run. One of the dudes that was sitting on a crate happen to look up just in time before Lil' Coon started spraying.

"OOOOH, Shit!" Was all he could get out of his mouth before a bullet hit him in the center of his forehead, spilling his brains all over the wall. By the way Lil' Coon and them were knocking them down, you would've thought it was just a movie, but this was real life. Sleep ran down on this dude who froze up like a deer caught in headlights. When the first bullet hit him, it knocked him totally off his feet, causing him to do a full back flip.

Everything that stood was falling like flies. It sounded like the 4th of July the way the highly powered rifles were letting off and knocking chunks of cement out of the store front. There was one guy who let loose a couple rounds while trying to make a run for it. It didn't work, though, because Lil' Coon was on his ass, firing round after round until a bullet struck him in the back and flipping him right out of his shoes. Then Coon ran up on another one, pointing the stick in his face and letting go another eight rounds, blowing his head right of his neck, before turning around and running towards the vehicle.

Bodies were laying on top of bodies. And the outside of the store was shot up so badly, you could see everything inside from the outside. Not too far from where the murders took place, Coon and the gang reloaded their weapons while leaving the scene. Shortly after, they pulled up to the housing projects.

Around this time of night, the projects be live as usual, hustlers selling to junkies without a care in the world, but tonight would be a lil' different.

Sleep pulled up and they all jumped out without being seen. Some cat was standing behind the garbage can, counting money, when all four circled everybody off. The cat behind the garbage can was the first person who got it. Head shots was the only target as Lil' Coon let off the first round, hitting dude behind the garbage can point blank.

Dude's head exploded like a watermelon; he was already dead before his body hit the ground. Gunshots erupted from the four gunmen as they chopped everything that was alive in the blank of an eye.

***

Days Later

Myesha was giving Lil' Coon a back massage when out the blue, the front door to their house got kicked in.

Boom! The front door flew open.

"Police! Everybody gets on the fucking ground!" the law enforcers yelled while running towards Lil' Coon and Myesha with their pistols and assault rifles out.

Five minutes later, the police officers were escorting Lil' Coon out the house in handcuffs before throwing in the in the back of the patrol car, before pulling off.

Once at the police station, they put Lil' Coon in a cold ass room for hours before two detectives entered. One of them had a folder in his hand, slamming it down, making the photo that was inside scatter across the table.

"Twenty-three muthafuckin bodies in one night you son of a bitch. How can you explain dis!?" The detective pushed the photos of the dead victims in front of Lil' Coon to look at. All Lil' Coon did was sit with his arms folded across his chest as he looked at the photos.

"Okay... wat da fuck you showing me pictures of dead peoples for? The only dead peoples dat I get alone wit, is da ones dats in my pocket."

"Oh, so you wanna be a wise guy, you dick face? We'll see if its funny when yo' punk ass be sitting in prison for the rest of your natural black ass life, if you don't tell me what I wanna know."

"Muthafucka, I wanna know who's responsible for

these murders 'cause if you don't come clean somebody's gonna take the wrap, and that person's gonna be you." At that very moment, a knock came from the door before it swung opened, and I'll be damned! In walks Lil' Coon's attorney.

First question he asked, "Is my client being charged with anything? If not, let him go now," he said. His attorney was an extremely high-priced defense advocate. Everyone knew he was a powerful man that was great at what he did. Even the D.A.'s office representatives were afraid to go up against him in court. He was the type of counselor that never lost a case.

"Well, sir, this is a very serious matter. We have reason to believe that your client was either the shooter or and accessory the situation at hand."

Lil' Coon's attorney responded by asking them what kind of information or proof they must have to prove the accusations. The best part of it is when he asked them to bring forth the evidence. Then he continued by stating, "If not, then you all are just holding my client against his own free will. Let's not forget that is a violation of the 4th and 6th constitutional amendment rights."

Within twenty-five minutes, Lil' Coon was walking away a free man. Myesha had been waiting in the parking lot the whole time for her king to be released. The two detectives watched them the entire time with hatred and evilness in their eyes. The man that was liable for all twenty-three bodies was walking away free. Everybody from Lauderdale was trying to communicate with Coon to let him know that they weren't the ones responsible for the shooting, and they had nothing to do with the fact that K-Dog was in a coma. That was like talking to a brick wall.

In addition, trap doors were being kicked in and invaded on every block. Body counts were piling up on all streets. Even the FBI and the DEA's were trying to put an end to the madness. But, the only way to conclude the reckless behavior was to catch Lil' Coon red-handed. He knew they were watching so he laid back and let his crew make all the moves.

Someone came clean or else the killing would've still been occurring, For the last six months the Take Over crew created havoc on the streets. But, still not a single soul came forward with any information concerning the shooter that was involved with K-Dog. Lil' Coon decided to take Myesha to South Carolina where his father lived. It was just to get away from everything that was going on. Killa taught Lil' Coon well, and even though he was no longer part of the game, he still instructed Lil' Coon on how to move in the streets.

One Hand Washed the Other
Killa
One Month Later
CHAPTER 27

Since K-Dog was in the hospital, Killa took over the car lot. It's already been a year and K-Dog still hadn't pulled out of the coma yet. That's what was fucking with Killa's head bad. The shoe was now on the other foot. Killa knew exactly what K-Dog was going through being in oblivion.

The hospital had informed him that everything was going ok with K-Dog. He was just in a deep sleep and it was up to him if he wanted to wake up or not. In other words, choose life or death. Deep down inside, Killa knew K-Dog would pull through, though. He was one survivor, that had lots to lose.

With all the killing Lil' Coon and the crew did, Killa still had a gut feeling that they didn't get the person that was responsible for running down on his best friend. Killa didn't want to go back to the streets, but he knew he had to play a part in this one. K-Dog was his right-hand man, and he knew that if the shoe was on the other foot that K-Dog would do the same for him.

Today was Memorial Day and Fort Lauderdale Beach was packed with residents and tourists from all over. Killa and the other members of the Take Over team decided to hit the strip. The sun was bright so when it hit the candy colored paints on their cars, it almost looked edible. Bitches started jumping out of their vehicles, trying to get pictures with the crew. All those females either had their tongues or their asses out while taking the pics. Lil' Coon always had to be the one to steal the show. That's what made every female want a piece of him. Just so they could go back and tell their homegirls.

The Take Over team was posted in the parking lot, standing next to their tricked-out rides. They were about fifty deep. All of them were wearing designer clothing with the flashiest fine jewelry. Weed aroma was in the air and bottles of Remy Martin V.S.O.P were being popped open. Of course, you still had niggas shooting dice, but today would be a day everyone remembered.

Meanwhile, Killa was sitting on top of his '73 donk, that sat on 30's, with Dominique and Bray. The three of them enjoyed themselves while watching all the activities. Then out of the blue, some bad bitches walked in front of them with Precious as the lead.

"Hey baby daddy, you act like you don't know a bitch," Precious said with her hands on her hips. "Can we talk?"

"About what Precious?" Killa asked.

"Boy, why you keep doing me like this after all I went through behind yo' ass?" she snapped.

Killa felt himself getting agitated so he said, "Look, Precious, if it's not about Rayanna, then I don't want anything to do with you besides the fact that I wish you well."

Precious became even more hostile. Then she said, "Aight! Since that's how you want to play it, I got something for yo' ass, watch!" Then she stormed off with her friends, following a few steps behind.

"Dat girl got some reeeeallll issues," Bray said, walking over to the cooler and grabbing two wine coolers. Lil' Coon was standing there as well.

"Dominique, girl, you want one of these?"

"Yeah, girl, I guess. Maybe this will help me take my mind off my baby. I miss him so much y'all," Dominique said, holding her head down.

"Girl, we know, you ain't the only person missing him either," Bray said, looking over at Killa, who wanted his right-hand man by his side on such a nice day like this one.

Killa began to think maybe if he was there at the time when the shooter ran down on K-Dog, then he wouldn't be where he was now. That's one of the reasons he even allowed Lil' Coon to spill so much blood in the first place. Around 6:00 p.m. the police started to run all the black people off the beach. Shit got out of control then. Bitches started fighting and bottles began to be used as weapons. Fort Lauderdale Police Department which we also called "city" had everything roped off. People were being escorted to the paddy wagon van for numerous types of charges. That still didn't stop them, though; it took for the Swat Team to come for everything to get under control.

***

Later that night, while Bray was sleeping, Killa and Lil' Coon was sitting in the front room of Killa's house, talking. Killa wanted to drop a few jewels on Lil' Coon just to keep him two steps ahead. Before he spoke, Killa picked up a blunt he had sitting in the ashtray on top of the glass table, lit it, then inhaled some smoke.

"I'm very proud of you, son. I watched you grow from

the time you were a youngin' up to the man that you are today," Killa said, exhaling the smoke through his nose. "And to be honest with you, Lil' Coon, I always knew you was gonna turn out this way. You are loyal, but very dangerous."

Lil' Coon smiled while taking the blunt from Killa. Then he continued, "But now is the time to start planning your future. Let me ask you a question lil' homie... where do you see yourself in the next ten years?"

Lil' Coon thought about the answer before speaking. Then he responded by saying, "Well, Yashua, we all have a vision whether if it's short-term or long-term. Ten years from now I'd be thirty-one. I see myself raising up a nation of black people, giving them jewels of knowledge dat will lead them on a straight and narrow path." Killa was impressed because he never heard Lil' Coon speak like that.

"A young Malcolm X, huh," Killa said, nodding in approval.

"Somethin' like dat, but more like being the leader of the black panthers," said Coon.

"Word to da wise, you can do anything you want and become somebody if you put yo' mind to it. Don't ever forget that."

"Now pass the weed, son." Then they burst out laughing.

A Blessing in Disguise
Lil' Coon
CHAPTER 28

A lot of people failed to realize you never judge a book by it's cover, let alone judge them by what they're wearing or what kind of car they drive. Even though Lil' Coon was who he was, he was still one of a kind. It's rare that you'd find another one in his age range like him. He was the true essence that most rappers talk about in their songs.

Lil' Coon grew up in a well-respected household raised by his grandmother, who was a god-fearing woman. When being born into this world of sin, his father had been serving time in a state penitentiary. Coon and his father never had that daddy-son relationship like most parents have with their children. The only time Lil' Coon got to see his father was when he was being punished. His father never showed him how to be a man. Any man can have a child, but it takes a real one to raise him up right.

His mother was a functional crack addict who taught him everything he knows. They were down like two flat tires. She loved him so dearly, it got to the point she never hid anything from him. Whenever she went, he went. Even when she went to buy dope, he was there right by her side. Around the age of thirteen he began to sell drugs, but he's been apart of a life of crime since he was about eight years old.

His uncle on his mother side used to take him on robberies with two other individuals. They would pull up on guys, jump out, and leave Lil' Coon alone in the car while they drew down on people. At the age of ten, Lil' Coon started breaking into houses and stealing vehicles, but his main hustle was stealing pit bulls. He would sell you the dog and then come back and steal it from you without you even knowing. To make matters worse, he dropped out of school in the 7th grade. His life was going downhill fast until Killa came into his life and changed everything.

Lil' Coon's favorite spot was the airport, because that was the one spot he could just let go and get away. He would look up at the planes as they took off, imagining leaving behind all the bullshit and never looking back. This was the only place he could get away and fantasize. He grew accustomed to it.

While Lil' Coon was sitting in his Bentley, watching the planes, an all-white BMW car pulled up and parked next to him. The driver of the car was a nice-looking female between the age 23-25. The whole time she was there, she watched the planes as they landed and took back off again. Coon could tell she looked good, but the only thing running through his mind was what she was doing out there in the first place. Could they share the same feelings, or could there be a very strong connection or what not? He just had to find out. Lil' Coon opened the door and got out, walking to the driver side of the vehicle and knocked on the window.

"Yes," the female said as she rolled down the window.

"Sorry to interrupt you, but I noticed you sitting alone over here, watching the planes and, I was wondering do you do dis on a regular?"

"Oh, my God, you caught me totally off guards with that one" she said, covering her mouth with her hands.

"Well, to be honest with you, my mother used to bring me here when I was just a little girl, and let's just say it stuck with me over the years. It's a reminder of my mother."

"Can I be honest with you and tell you sum'thin'?" Lil' Coon said.

"Of course, why not," Lil' Coon thought hard before saying.

"I come here from time to time. As a matter of fact, dis is one of my favorite spots."

"Really!"

"Yes." Lil' Coon smiled.

"WOW! Oh, by the way my name is Shavon," she said, reaching out her hand.

"It's nice to meet somebody that shares da same quality," Lil' Coon said, accepting her handshake.

"The pleasure is all mines," Shavon said, opening the car door to her vehicle and got out. Lil' Coon was surprise how fine and thick she was, Shavon was badder then what he expected.

Shavon looked Lil' Coon up and down from head to toe, admiring the jewels that were around his neck and wrist. Even the car he was driving, Shavon knew Lil' Coon was a boss.

"Can I ask you a question?" Shavon said.

"Yeah, go ahead, ask me anything," he replied.

"What's a person like you doin' driving something like that?" she said, pointing at the Bentley. "And how old are you?"

"Well, to answer yo' question, I'ma businessman and by the way, I'm only twenty-one years old."

"Very impressive," she said.

"And how old are you?" Lil' Coon asked.

"I'm twenty-four years old with no kids. I stay in a 3-bedroom house and I work at Bank of America," Shavon stated, hoping to be real Lil' Coon in with her accomplishments. "Wait! Pause for a moment," she said, only to look at a plane take off before speaking again. "I always wanted to know how it feels to sit in a Bentley."

Well, I can make that happen along with a lot of other things, all you gotta do is say the word," Lil' Coon said, walking towards his car and opening the door for Shavon to get in.

"Just like dat?" Shavon asked as she was sitting down in Lil' Coon's passenger seat.

"Yup! Just like that," Lil' Coon said, closing the door, then going around to the driver's side of the car and got in. "You smoke?" he asked her as he reached for the pre-rolled blunt, he had already sitting in his ashtray.

"Yes, I do."

With that said, Lil' Coon fired up the joint and hit it a few times before passing it to her. They both smoked the whole blunt while listening to Keith Sweat. Shavon was riding on cloud 9 while at the same time feeling horny.

"How does it feel to have sex in a Bentley?" She couldn't believe she just let that come out of her mouth, but she couldn't hep herself.

A smirked came across Lil' Coon's face before he said, "It's only one way to find out."

"Oh, really?" Shavon said, giving him the eye.

"Really," he responded.

That's all Shavon needed to hear. She took off her shirt and automatically unfastened her bra, letting her perfect c-cups take full view. Lil' Coon couldn't wait for her to fully undress. He reached over and started caressing her breasts while Shavon was taking off her pants, before they both climbed in the backseat.

"Come on, with yo' slow self," Shavon said, laughing out loud. The weed was really taking control over her.

Once Lil' Coon got undressed, he jumped in the backseat between her legs with a condom in his mouth.

"Oh, my God, I can't believe I'm doing this with a person I barely even know," she said, covering her face with both hands, in a shy-ish manner.

"Well, let's call this our little secret," Lil' Coon said before entering her.

Payback
Killa
CHAPTER 29

It's been another whole year and K-Dog was still in the coma. A lot had happened. Dominique had the little girl who was already very spoiled and always throwing temper tantrums if she didn't get what she wanted. She named her Diamond and she was spoiled rotten. Lil' Javon was growing up so fast it didn't make any sense. Unlike most firstborns, he automatically became attached to his baby sister. He was always by her side which was a good thing because it took a lot off Dominique's hands.

With all the murdering that's been taking place since K-Dog had been hospitalized Dominique knew in her heart who was the one behind it all. And she knew why it was happening too. She didn't approve of it, but at the same time, she also knew, there was nothing she could do to stop it. It was way beyond her reach.

As for Precious, she wanted payback for how Killa had betrayed her, and she knew the perfect plan. Right before Memorial Day, Precious made it her business to bump into Queen's boyfriend who they called, White Boy Bruce. He was the one that she was trying to get released from the Feds. Precious had some valuable information for him that would've been priceless. She knew who was responsible for killing his Queen.

Today was the day to put things into play. Precious waited patiently for this day to come. She was sitting inside the Denny's on Davie Blvd and 441, eating ice cream while talking on her cell phone. She was so caught up in her conversation she didn't even realized when White Boy Bruce was standing next to her. He startled her, when he tapped on her shoulder.

"Boy, what you doing sneaking up on people like you the damn police or something?" she quarreled while grabbing his head. "Have a seat before somebody see us."

"So, what's up?" White Boy Bruce said while being seated.

That's when Precious got straight to the point. "I know who's responsible for killing yo' girl Queen…"

***

Two Weeks Later

Killa was going to pick up Rayanna from Precious's apartment in Franklin Park called the Greens. Precious had called him, saying that their daughter was ready for him to come get her for the weekend as usual. Normally, around that time of evening, it be live outside. However, this specific night there wasn't a single soul out. It was very suspect when Killa turned on 18th and didn't see anybody. It made the hairs on the back of his neck stand up, but he brushed it off, thinking it's probably nothing and kept driving. In an instant, a blue and black car ran out right in front of him, forcing him to slam on the breaks.

"Get the fuck out my way!" Killa yelled, not paying any attention to the fact that this car looked familiar. But the cat just sat there, staring him dead in his eyes through the two tinted windshields. Somehow Killa caught movement out of his peripheral vision. When he looked, he noticed niggas was creeping up with choppas in their hands and using vehicles for cover. His instincts kicked in before the niggas was able to jump out on him. He threw his BMW X6 into reverse and hit the gas. Immediately, guns started going off.

Tat, tat, tat, tat… Tat, tat, tat, tat, tat… Tat, tat, tat… Tat, tat… Tat, tat, tat.

Bullets were hitting everything in sight and smashing out windshields. Killa drove out like a real trooper though, whipping it on 18th street before smashing out and getting ghost on they ass.

***

Two Days Later

A couple nights ago, when Killa tried to pick his daughter up from his baby moms house, someone tried to take his life away from him. The only reason he was still alive is thanks to the black cat. It was crazy because whoever was shooting wanted him gone. Bullet holes were in the headrest and everything. Could it had been the same person who ran down on K-Dog, was the same individual who was gunning at him? Or, could it be an enemy, pretending to be friend, laying down in the grass like a snake, waiting for the perfect time to strike?

Something in Killa's mind kept telling him that Precious was responsible. He refused to believe it, but he still put a member to follow her just to be sure. While he sat on the sofa, trying to put the pieces together, his phone started ringing. He answered saying.

"Hello?"

"Yashua..."

"Yea, wats up, bruh?" Killa said.

"Man, I got some shit to tell you," the person said.

"I'm listening," Killa said, sitting straight up in his seat as if he knew what was about to be said.

"Slide on me, bruh," his homeboy told him.

"Say no more, where you at?" Killa asked.

"Meet me at the spot in twenty minutes."

"That?"

"That!" his friend said, ending the call.

Killa, Lil' Coon, and Sleep were already at the spot when the member who had information arrived. As they sat down at the round table together, the member was shaking his head because the news he was about to tell Killa would fuck him up in the worse way.

"What's good, John-John?" Killa asked, getting to the point.

"Bruh, Precious is fuckin wit' White Boy Bruce. I followed her to Lauderhill mall, and I saw her get out of her car and into his."

"You talkin' about Queen's peoples?" Lil' Coon asked with firm ears.

"Yea, but what made it more fucked up was the fact that I saw her giving him head before she got out and left," John-John spoke.

Killa couldn't believe the bullshit that just ran in and out of his ears. Was the bitch really trying to get him whacked? Killa begun to replay everything in his head, and it all started making sense.

"Damn! I can't believe this bitch would really go this far to try and take a nigga out the game." Killa shook his head in awe. Then, he hit the table, almost flipping it over. Lil' Coon even started to feel some type of way because he was trying to figure out, why in the hell would Precious do some shit like that?

John-John finished off by telling Killa, "From my understanding, it wasn't meant for you to make it out alive brotha."

"You know what Lil' Coon, now that I think about it, you're right!" Killa was seeking revenge in an evil manner. "Aight, check this out y'all boys... this how I want it to go down," he said, coming up with a plan.

**

Killa wanted to kill two birds with one stone by running down on them while they were with each other. It had been a whole week since the crew was able to catch them both together. Lil' Coon and Sleep were sitting outside of Sky Hotel, waiting for Killa to arrive. It was only fifteen minutes before he ended up pulling into the parking lot. Both Lil' Coon and Sleep exited the vehicles as they waited for Killa to do the same. Lil' Coon didn't speak to Killa once he came out of the car, the only thing he did was nod his head before walking in the direction of the room where Precious and White Boy Bruce was.

Lil' Coon had already gotten everything set up when they stood outside the room door. He paid the maid, whom he'd been fucking, about a grand to give him the room key. Once they were all in position, Lil' Coon placed the key card in the slot and waited for the light to turn green, before opening it.

Precious and White Boy Bruce was in a 69 position, getting their freak on. They were so caught up in the moment that they didn't see death right in front of them, until Lil' Coon cocked back his pistol.

Click clack! The gun sounded.

White Boy Bruce was in so much of a shock he didn't

know what to do.

"What the fuck?" he said, looking up and seeing three gunmen, standing above them. He turned and looked at Precious, who was also in shock, and said, "Bitch, you set me up?"

"Aye bruh, look…," White Boy Bruce said, holding his hands up. "It was all her fault; I swear on everything, I love. She called me talking about she knew who killed Queen, etc."

This Muthafucka turned the whole story around, putting everything on Precious. Killa looked at Lil' Coon and Sleep, giving them the okay. The both of them walked over to White Boy Bruce and pointed their guns at him, which had silencers on them by the way, and emptied the clips in him before stepping to the side, allowing Killa to approach. Killa had no words for Precious as she tried to plead for her life. The only he said before putting two bullets in her skull was, "I'll make sure Rayanna won't forget about you."

Sleeping Next to the Enemy
K-Dog
CHAPTER 30

It's now officially been 3 ½ years since K-Dog's been in the coma. The doctor said he wasn't sure if he would pull through. One of the nurses at the hospital noticed him moving, when she was doing her rounds. Could it have been that her eyes were playing tricks on her? The nurse had no other choice but to check and see if everything was alright with him.

An hour later, K-Dog's eyes opened and started blinking, his vision was blurry as he looked around, not realizing where he was. It took him a minute or two for his vision to adjust to his surroundings. That's when he was able to see and realized he was in the hospital. The nurse let K-Dog adjust to his surroundings before making her presence known.

"Hello, Mr. Williams, my name is Latia. Do you know where you're at?" K-Dog looked around before shaking his head.

"Very good, Mr. Williams," she said. Then she asked him if he would like to have a drink of water.

"Yes," K-Dog said very low in a raspy tone.

After nurse Latia gave K-Dog a drink of water, she explained everything to him about why he was in the hospital. It was kind of sad because he didn't remember any of it. The bodyguards that stood outside of K-Dog's door called Killa when they found out that he woke up.

Within thirty minutes, the hospital was packed with friends and loved ones. When Dominique arrived at the hospital, she surprised the hell out of K-Dog with Diamond in her arms. Lil' Javon was so glad to see his father out of the coma; all he could do was talk to him about all the things that had happened since.

Killa, Lil' Coon, and the rest of the Take Over crew were also there. However, now that he was awake the only thing on their minds were on was who was the person that was behind the trigger.

Later that night after everyone left, Killa and Lil' Coon stayed back to have a talk with K-Dog. K-Dog knew what they wanted, but he couldn't give them the answers that they were looking for because he honestly didn't remember a thing. Killa explained everything to K-Dog about how Lil' Coon and a few others went on a rampage bodying over forty niggas. Then he told him about how Precious tried to set him up to get killed by White Boy Bruce.

While they were talking, the nurse entered the room to inform them that visiting hours were officially over. Before leaving, Lil' Coon lifted his shirt and pulled out a gun. He gave it to K-Dog before turning around and walking out the door. "Keep that just in big homie," was the last thing he said before leaving K-Dog's side.

***

As K-Dog slept, he heard a lot of noise coming from behind the curtain in his room. All he heard was screaming and by the sound of it, he knew the person was really in a lot of pain. A few moments later, the screaming completely stopped. K-Dog listen closely, overhearing a doctor, mentioning how the person who was behind the curtains was shot up pretty good. That was the only thing K-Dog remembered before drifting off to sleep.

Around 8:00 o'clock in the morning, the person who were on the other side of the curtain was having a visit. From the sound of it the individual was only a kid, who been shot three times. As K-Dog began to think to himself, a nurse came through the door with a cart.

"Breakfast time," she said. As soon as he heard this, he sat up in the bed, rubbing his hands together. K-Dog was starving.

"What are we having today, Latia?" he asked.

"Cheese grits, eggs, beef sausage, and toast," nurse Latia responded.

By the sound of it, K-Dog knew that breakfast was going to be delicious. He couldn't wait to dig in as soon as the nurse gave him the plate. The first bite he took K-Dog couldn't believe how awful the food tasted.

"What the fuck is this shit?" K-Dog said while spitting the food back out unto the tray. The nurse had already exited the room, so he couldn't complain. This shit is unbelievable, K-Dog thought to himself, as he got out of the bed and walked out the room. When the bodyguards saw him, they rushed to his side.

"Wuz up boss, what can we do for you?" one asked.

K-Dog responded by saying, "I want some real food. This shit they just gave me tastes like rubber."

"Don't worry about it, we'll take care of it. Anything else you need?" said the guard.

"Naw, that's it for now," said K-Dog with thanks in his tone.

While K-Dog was standing outside his room, the visitors that had come for the kid were leaving out. K-Dog walked back inside and caught a glimpse of the kid walked back towards his bed. Once he got back in bed and laid down, they both acknowledged one another. Forty-five minutes later, the bodyguard came back in with so much food that it looked like he robbed a whole restaurant.

"Well, damn, Chris, what did you do? Look like you stuck up the people for all this food," K-Dog said with a slight laughter.

"Naw, man. I know you haven't eaten in years, so I'm just tryna make sure you get ya weight back up," said bodyguard Chris.

"I appreciate it, man," K-Dog said.

"No problem, man, if you need anything else just holla," Chris responded before exiting the room.

"Aight, bet!"

Once Chris left, K-Dog immediately started digging into the food like a wild pig who hadn't eaten in weeks. He was smacking out loud and everything. It had gotten to the point that the kid on the other side of the curtain couldn't stand it any longer. He snatched the curtains back and just looked at K-Dog, as he ate like a mad man. The kid wanted to snap, but seeing how he was eating. He instead said, "You look like you haven't eaten in weeks."

"Try years," K-Dog said with a mouth full of food. By the look on the kids face. K-Dog could tell that he was also hungry. "You want some of this food? It tastes way better than the shit you have sitting next to you," he offered.

"Hell yeah, I want some. I haven't eaten in two days," said the kid. K-Dog passed him the bags he hadn't touched yet. As they ate, the room got so quiet you would've heard a rat pissed on cotton. After they finished eating, the kid informed K-Dog on how he was trapping, and two armed men kicked the door in and shot him three times before leaving. The conversation went on for hours.

K-Dog was beginning to like the kid because he reminded him so much of how he used to be. What surprised him the most was the fact that the kid pulled a Glock 40 from under his pillow and pointed it at K-Dog, as he demonstrated and displayed the red beam that was attached to it. The kid knew that K-Dog was someone important because of how the guards were set up outside. But somehow, he also found something familiar in K-Dog, he just couldn't put his finger on it.

That night nurse Latia was on duty that came to check on them before turning the lights out. K-Dog and the kid stayed up until the wee hours of the morning talking about life. Mainly it was K-Dog who did the talking, though, but the kid didn't mind.

"See, young blood, this game we livin' in don't last foreva. You've gotta calculate every move like chess. You get in, make the money, then invest it in your own business. Where we go wrong is 'cause we get blinded and start tryna make a career outta the game." K-Dog said. He went on for hours, giving the kid advice and pointers about the game, hoping he wouldn't make the same mistakes he did.

Even though the kid was already out there slanging and banging in the streets. He never had anyone drop them jewels on him like K-Dog was doing. So, it was only right that he opened up and explained to K-Dog what was really going on in his life. "I appreciate you breaking down the rules of the game to me. It means a lot. I never meant to be in this game, but life has its twists and turns, you know. When my father got murdered, I was only a child, so I ain't eva get to bond wit 'em or anything. My mama used to show me pictures of him all the time and shit," said the kid. His emotions were starting to get the best of him. Tears started falling from his eyes.

"How was your father murdered?" K-Dog asked, feeling sorry for him.

"Somebody had shot him in the head," the kid said. Then he continued. "But you know, though, I made it my business to find that Muthafucka when I got older, and when I did, I emptied the whole clip in him before I stood over him and watched him take his last breaths."

"You know what young blood; I don't even know your name. What is yo' name?"

"Percy, I was named after my father," he said.

K-Dog thought to himself. That name sounded familiar. He just couldn't put his finger on it, but the name was ringing bells like a high school fire alarm.

"You know what?" Percy said.

"Wuz that?" said K-Dog.

"You look familiar, man, I swear to God," Percy said, examining K-Dog. "Do you own any businesses?" he asked.

"As a matter of fact, I do," K-Dog answered while still trying to think about why all of this sounds so familiar.

"Do you own a car lot?"

"Yes!"

3 ½ years ago, Percy ran down on a man that was responsible for killing his father, but it couldn't have been K-Dog because Percy made sure that the man that killed his father was dead. Could it be that he made it out alive, or could it have been a coincidence that maybe K-Dog had a car lot too, like the man who he murdered cold blood.

Both of their medications were kicking in, so sleep begun to take over. As their bodies gave in to the powerful drugs, they began slumber like newborn babies. They were both dreaming as well. K-Dog was having the same dream of before he was shot, but this time his dreams were replaying the events that took place at the car lot.

Percy's dream was also replaying the day he ran down on the dude who killed his father. The face of the guy responsible was becoming clearer and clearer as he fought to get a better look. Within a couple minutes, the face of the person laying down came into full view. It couldn't be, it's impossible. The person's face in his dream was also the person laying next to him. It was no one other than K-Dog.

At the same time, K-Dog's dreams were starting to make sense. The person who stood over him face became bright as the sun in the early morning. It was nobody else but Percy. Just then, they both woke up at the same time and grabbed their pistols. They pointed them at one another with nothing but pure murder in their eyes.

TO BE CONTINUED….

Made in the USA
Columbia, SC
22 November 2024

47004046R00102